A Small Town Christmas

A Small Town Christmas

A Four Irish Brother Winery Romance

Nan Reinhardt

TULE
PUBLISHING

For Lizzie, who always believes in me, is the best writing buddy ever, and who made me believe in this book even when I couldn't see the end. Thank you, ma chére amie.

Chapter One

IT WAS ALL Millie's fault. The roadside sign—*Millie's Pie Emporium*—had enticed Samantha Hayes off the interstate and onto the country road where she was now stranded. In spite of the flat tire and the pouring rain, she smiled, remembering the delicious slice of pecan pie she'd had at Millie's, along with amazing chicken and dumplings, fresh peas, and biscuits that were pure poetry.

Her mother would scoff at taking a detour for something as mundane as pie, but then she'd never been a foodie like Sam. Mother ate for fuel, nothing more, while Sam ate purely for pleasure. Her friend Suz hated the fact Sam could eat like a trucker and remain slim and had warned her since eighth grade that one day her hummingbird metabolism would give out.

Just last week at their monthly lunch, Suz shook her head as Sam scarfed down a double-fudge chocolate sundae while Suz primly spooned up a single scoop of low-fat vanilla. "Just you wait 'til menopause. It's gonna getcha, girl, and all that sugar and fat will land right on your tiny behind."

Sam wasn't worried. She came from a long line of hardy Hayes women, who ate whatever they wanted and lived to be lean, wiry senior citizens. *Just look at Aunt Bette.* Besides, menopause was years away. She gave a quick glance in the rearview mirror. Worried dark brown eyes under a thick fringe of auburn hair looked back at her. Thirty-two didn't seem bad at all; her skin was smooth and soft. High cheekbones emphasized the fact that, somewhere in the distant past, one of her Irish ancestors had taken a Shawnee bride.

However, none of that changed the fact she was stuck on the side of a two-lane highway in the hills of southern Indiana. Rain pounded on the roof and drizzled down the windshield while the *swipe, swish, swipe, swish* of the wipers gave her brief views of the late fall landscape. Trees had dropped most of their leaves, creating a colorful red, orange, and yellow border in the grass along the shoulder. The air smelled crisp, yet a little musty, and the chill, creeping in since she'd turned off her heater, made her shiver. She glanced behind her, but there was nothing to see except more bare trees and a long empty road. Flicking on the hazard lights, she rested her forehead on the steering wheel and moaned.

The sun had been shining across the Chicago River when she'd left the city late that Sunday morning. The mechanic at the dealership had assured her the car was in great shape when she'd had the routine service done on it only last week. Oil changed, tires rotated, fluid levels checked, and a complementary detailing to celebrate her fifth year of BMW ownership.

It had been her first brand-new car—a gift from her aunt Bette when Sam had passed the bar—and she'd secretly named the sports coupe Gigi because of the cutesy voice that gave her directions when she turned on the navigation. For nearly five years, she'd treated it as lovingly as a mother treated a child. And how did the silly thing repay all her years of careful maintenance? By getting a flat in the middle of some dismal road, less than thirty minutes away from her destination.

And in the rain.

A semi sped by, splashing water all over the side of the car and drawing Sam's attention back to her situation. Time to focus and figure out what she was going to do. The rain pelting down showed no sign of letting up any time soon and even though it was only early afternoon, she longed to be warm and snug in the B&B her assistant had booked her into in River's Edge—the photos on the web showed rooms with cozy fireplaces and colorful quilts. She found her umbrella in the console and got out, sending up an arrow prayer that the tire might be drivable.

Apparently, the angels were busy elsewhere because the right front tire wasn't just flat, it was shredded.

How did that happen?

With a sigh, Sam climbed back in, took up her cell phone, and gazed at the screen. At least she had a couple of bars of service and the 4G seemed to be working. Great news if she had even a clue whom to call. She certainly wasn't going to call the winery where she was headed to do business—how unprofessional would that be? The attorney who was supposed to be saving this family business stranded on a back road? No, especially not when this was her first big non-divorce case. Her chance to show her boss she could do other kinds of lawyering. A touch of the screen brought the GPS to life and showed her exactly where she was, only fifteen miles from River's Edge, so she asked the phone to find her a garage or gas station nearby.

Gus's Service Station was in Cedar Hill, the next town south. She dialed the number and was greeted with a gruff, "Garage."

When Sam explained her dilemma, the man on the other end of the line guffawed. "Lady, I got four calls ahead of you and only two tow trucks. I can get there in mebbe two, three hours. You're gonna have to sit tight."

"Is there anyone else I can call?" She chewed her lower lip. Fog on the windows told her the temperature was dropping. She shouldn't have let the emergency roadside service that came with her car lapse, but she hardly ever drove out of Chicago, so she hadn't bothered with renewing. Dammit.

"Nope. Even if you got Triple A, I'm the one they call around here."

"But I've got to get to River's Edge and—"

"Lady, we all gotta get somewhere. Now, my tale of woe is that my nephew took off last night with the mayor's daughter *and* my sister's brand-new Land Rover. The only other guys I got to drive tow trucks for me are a sixteen-year-old who doesn't know one end of a wrench from the other and my worthless brother-in-law, who ain't no mechanic either, but he can probably change a tire." He gave a disgusted snort of laughter. "He's out on a call west o' town and the kid's down to McHenryville pulling a tractor outta the mud."

"I'm really sorry, but I'm all alone out here and I've got a really important meeting tomorrow morning at nine." Sam didn't play defenseless well, but it was worth a shot; maybe she could elicit some sympathy from Gus. A cheap tactic, but one she wasn't above using at this point.

"An important meeting, huh? Well, now that's an entirely different story." Gus's sarcasm came through loud and clear, even with only two bars. It was looking very likely she was going to be changing her own tire in the rain.

She swallowed a sharp retort. Responding in kind to the man's rudeness was not going to get her tire changed. "I'd truly appreciate some help, sir."

"Look, just tell me again where you are and I'll get someone out there soon as I can."

Sam went ahead and gave him the information from her GPS, managing to be halfway polite when once again he ordered her to "sit tight." It was a wretched day weather-wise and that wasn't his fault. Neither was her flat tire. Gus sounded as overwhelmed as she felt. She clicked off and dialed the B&B to let them know she was going to be a late check-in, but got no answer, so she left a message. She debated for about three minutes before reaching into the back seat for her raincoat, figuring she might as well get out and fix the darn tire. She'd been changing tires since she'd gotten her license at sixteen, so she had no excuse except her own unwillingness to get wet.

CONOR FLAHERTY SQUINTED through the rain-blurred windshield, slowed to a crawl, and muttered a curse. Some idiot had pulled over to the side of the road, but not far enough. The back end of a sporty little vehicle stuck out over the edge of the pavement and he had to veer into the opposite lane to avoid it. He crept past and did a double-take at the scene before him.

The car's hazard lights were blinking, and a drenched woman bent over the open trunk, clearly struggling with the spare tire. He pulled his SUV off the highway in front of the cockeyed sports car. He could see the shredded right front tire when he glanced in the rearview mirror.

"Guess we'd better see if we can lend a hand. Hold down the fort, Ali," he said as he zipped up his jacket and grabbed the cap from the seat beside him. "I'm going to see if I can help this lady, okay?"

Alannah's dark eyes widened, but Conor gave her a reassuring smile before reaching back to check the safety harness on his daughter's car seat. "It'll be okay, honey. I'm just going to be right back there, helping this lady fix her tire." When the little girl's lip quivered, Conor stroked her hair and ran a finger down her chubby cheek. "It's all good, baby. Here's Mabel"—he handed Alannah a tattered stuffed rabbit—"and here's your book." He opened Richard Scarry's *What Do People Do All Day*, Ali's current favorite. "Find all the firefighters and when I come back, you can show me, okay?"

"Da . . ." Ali gave the slightest nod, but fear shadowed her eyes, so he started the car, checked the traffic in his side mirror, and pulled away. A couple hundred feet up the road, he checked traffic again and did a one-eighty, heading back to the woman in distress. When he pulled over this time and shut off the engine, he faced the front of her car. "Look, see that car up there?"

Ali nodded, craning her neck to peer out the front window from her spot in the center of the back seat. She got motion sick in the car, but Conor had figured out that if the car seat was in the middle and she could see out the front window, the kid was less likely to be nauseated. Plus, he always kept a supply of airsick bags handy. He got out, pocketed the car keys, and opened the back door to lean in and pick up the book Ali had dropped during the U-turn.

"See her tire? It's flat and she can't drive, so I'm going to see if I can help." He turned some pages. "You can watch and you'll see me almost the whole time. I'll only disappear when I go to get her tire out, but count to twenty when you don't see me and I'll be right back in view."

Alannah nodded, her expression now more curious than fearful. He dropped a kiss on the top of her head. "I won't be long, love."

She nodded again and, with that, Conor trudged through the rain, which had now subsided to a chilly drizzle. As he drew closer to the car, the air was fairly blue with the woman's frustration and he couldn't help grinning as he approached the back of the vehicle. "Can I help you?"

"Oh, crap." When she released the handle of the cable holding the tire, her foot slid on the wet gravel and her arms wheeled as she tried to keep herself upright.

He bolted around the rear fender and caught her just before she hit the ground. He kept an arm around her waist to steady her. "You okay?"

She was tall, really tall. Her high-heeled boots were completely inappropriate for the wet gravel, let alone for changing a tire, and they made her seem even taller—their eyes were nearly level.

"I'm fine, you just startled me," she grumbled and stepped away from him to plop down on the bumper with a grimace. "Oh . . . and thanks." The hood of her raincoat had fallen back, revealing a mass of dark auburn curls. When she shoved her fingers through them and he finally saw her face,

8

her cheeks were rosy, either from the cold or embarrassment, and her eyes signaled that she was beyond frustrated. "I can't get the damn . . . er, darn tire to drop. It's stuck."

He gave her a smile. "Want me to give it a try?"

She moved aside with a sweeping gesture. "Be my guest."

Conor tugged on the cable handle—the tire didn't move an inch—it *was* stuck under the storage compartment. He allowed the tiniest moment of self-flagellation for assuming the problem was that a woman couldn't get a spare out from under the trunk of a car while he examined the small compartment, trying to remember what he knew about this particular vehicle. "A-ha," he exclaimed. "There's another nut, see? Here under the cable. Let's try that." He sent a thankful prayer heavenward for his brother, Aidan's, expensive taste in cars as he loosened the nut, pinched the lock clip, and held the cable while the tire carrier eased to the ground below the trunk.

"I watched the video twice before I even opened the trunk. How'd I miss that step?" The woman rolled her eyes, the deepest chocolate brown Conor had ever seen. Even darker than Ali's. If he'd been born a poet he might have been able to come up with a more lyrical analogy, but he wasn't a poet, and the thought of chocolate reminded him Ali was probably hungry. Besides, he hadn't waxed poetic about a woman in over two years—not since Emmy died.

Best to just get this done, so they could get home to supper.

"Changing tires on these European models is trickier

than on American cars." He pulled the tire from its carrier and rolled it around the side of the car.

"Why did you come back?" she asked suddenly as she followed him.

"What?"

"You left and then you came back." She handed him the tire iron and he inserted it in the jack she had placed perfectly under the frame near the front tire. "Why?"

"Oh, I didn't leave." The question was unexpected. He would've guessed she hadn't even noticed him drive up; she was so involved in struggling with her tire. "I just turned my car around so my daughter could watch me. She . . . um, she needs to see me." He pointed with the tire iron. He wasn't exactly sure why he felt the need to explain, but something about her frank inquisitive gaze invited that small confidence.

She peered through the drizzle and then offered Ali a hesitant wave, before giving Conor a nod and a small frown. "Is she okay? Should I maybe go sit with her or something?" She pulled her hood back up over her hair with a quick snap of fabric that sent an unexpected wash of regret through him.

"Thanks, but she'll be fine as long as she can see me." He blinked, shook his head, and focused on changing the tire, loosening lug nuts that were so tight they'd obviously been put on with air tools. The woman wasn't frail, but she certainly would've had trouble getting them off by herself, although he respected the fact she'd been willing to try.

She leaned on the front fender as he worked on the tire, quietly staying out of the way. Nevertheless, he was very aware of her. When he took off the old shredded tire, she hauled it to the rear of the car and had it secured in the carrier and back up under the trunk when he got there with the jack and the rest of the tools. They reloaded the car together and after she slammed the trunk lid down, she stepped away from behind the vehicle.

Conor came around, too, surprised she'd made a point to move to a place where Ali could see them, but grateful at the same time. How nice she was aware enough of children to understand the shred of information he'd revealed about his daughter. Surreptitiously, he checked the contents of her vehicle but didn't see anything that might've belonged to a child and she was clearly way too young to have adult kids. He'd set a small suitcase back into the trunk, and the expensive-looking leather satchel on the back seat might hold a laptop and important papers, while a suit covered in dry-cleaner's plastic hung on the hook by the window. Obviously, she was traveling.

But to where? And from where?

Why was he even wondering? It wasn't like he was ever going to see her again and asking would just mean a delaying conversation. She hadn't been terribly forthcoming anyway.

She stuck out her hand. "Thank you. I appreciate this more than you know. May I . . . may I pay you for your trouble?"

Conor glanced over at Ali, who had lost interest in her dad and was busy scanning the pages in her book. He shook the woman's hand briskly because, for some unknown reason, what he wanted to do was hug her. What the heck was going on with him? "It was no problem." When she didn't reply, but simply regarded him with those big brown eyes, his discomfiture increased, so he turned toward his own car. "Be safe driving to . . . well, be safe," he called over his shoulder.

A FRISSON OF disappointment fluttered through Sam as the man walked away, and she nearly called out "River's Edge!" before she remembered that, but for this small kindness, he was a complete stranger. He hadn't offered his name and she hadn't asked for it. Then again, he hadn't asked hers, either. It had been an oddly formal encounter given the situation. Not that it mattered. She'd never see him again anyway.

But she stood by her car door, gazing, as he leaned into the backseat to check on his daughter. It warmed Sam's heart to see how solicitous he was—as far as she was concerned, nothing was more attractive than a good father. As an attorney who dealt primarily with family law, she'd seen too many who weren't. From this distance, she couldn't tell how old the child was, but she was still in a car seat, so probably younger than eight.

When the guy stayed in the backseat for longer than seemed necessary, Sam wondered if the little girl was okay. She squinted through the misty rain, not sure if she should step up and check on them. However, it appeared the two were merely sitting there paging through a book, so she unzipped her now thoroughly soaked Burberry raincoat, slipped it off, gave it a quick shake, and tossed it into the backseat. Eyeing the pair in the SUV, she climbed into her car and started the engine, letting the defroster clear the windows that had clouded over.

While she waited, she dialed Gus to let him know she no longer needed his services and chose to smile rather than be offended by his "Good for you, little lady" response. This was small-town life and she'd do well to come in with a smile and good attitude. After all, her new client lived in a very small town—River's Edge, Indiana—named appropriately enough because it sat smack on the Ohio River.

By the time the windshield had cleared, the man who'd helped her was in the driver's seat of his SUV and steam emanated from the tailpipe, but he was still sitting on the side of the road. Suddenly it occurred to her he was probably waiting for her to take off—that would be the gentlemanly thing to do and, unquestionably, he was a gentleman. She put the car in gear, checked her mirrors for traffic, and pulled out. As she passed him, she gave him a wave and a smile and he tapped his horn, a quick *beep* of acknowledgement.

Chapter Two

MONDAY MORNING HADN'T started out well. Conor overslept, which meant shoving Ali through breakfast and getting dressed for preschool. Tears ensued when they realized he hadn't gotten the laundry done last night and Ali's favorite purple shirt wasn't clean. He'd spent valuable minutes convincing her the orange shirt was perfect for the post-Thanksgiving return to school—pumpkins and all that—and even managed to get her braid relatively tidy in spite of rushing. He was always amazed when that happened. Emmy had been brilliant at French braiding, turning out a perfect plait every time—not only with Ali's baby-fine hair, but with her own thick tresses as well. She'd worked with him those last few months, guiding his clumsy fingers while Ali sat still as a mouse on the side of the hospital bed he'd set up in the living room for her mom.

By the time he'd loaded Ali into the car to head to pre-school, she was sunny again and anxious to tell her teacher all about yesterday's adventure helping a stranded motorist, although she was somewhat exasperated with her father because he didn't know the lady's name. She had gasped in four-year-old horror at his suggestion that *she* make up a name for the tall young woman who'd stayed in his head long after they'd gone their separate ways.

"Da!" Ali scowled when he'd glanced in the rearview mirror. "What if we see her again and call her by the pretend name and she thinks we're silly and won't talk to us?"

"I doubt we'll see her again." Conor smiled and shook his head. "We could just call her the mystery lady."

"Or the car trouble lady," Ali suggested, getting into the spirit of the game.

"That's good, too."

"What about the really, really wet lady?" Ali's laughter pierced Conor's heart. Even at this young age, she already sounded so much like Emmy when she laughed.

God, how I miss her.

They played the name game until he pulled into the pre-school lot and bundled her into her jacket and hat. The weather had turned downright cold after last night's rain and he felt around in Ali's pockets for her mittens. "Be sure to put these on if you go outside today, okay?"

"Okay." She was already distracted, clearly anxious to get into the building to play with her friends. "Come on, Da. Miss Karen's mommy is bringing in kittens today." Ali tugged at his hand. "I can't wait to pet one. I love kitties, don't you?"

Conor rolled his eyes, hoping Miss Karen's mommy wasn't expecting any of the parents to take a kitten home with them when they picked up their kids. Zin and Merlot, the two cats who lived at the winery took care of the critter problem just fine. He wasn't up for introducing any new animals into their lives right now.

The Monday after Thanksgiving was generally a day when he took a breath and got the winery back to normal before the holiday rush began the following weekend. The tasting room in town needed to be restocked, a shipment of new bottles was due around noon, he had to hit the bank with the deposits from the long weekend, and, oh damn, there was that meeting with the attorney Sean had set up.

What is that guy's name again?

He pulled out his phone to check his calendar before he started the SUV. Scrolling to the week view, he found it. *Sam Hayes 9:00 A.M.* He had a little over an hour to get back, make some coffee, and find the paperwork he needed for the meeting.

His phone rang as he started the car and he pressed the button on the steering wheel to talk to his oldest brother. "Hiya, Sean."

"How'd the weekend go?" Sean's booming voice filled the car.

"It was good. Got a tidy sum to deposit today and we sold enough in town that I've got to restock before we open up again tomorrow." Conor pulled out of the lot and headed into the hills above River's Edge. "Nobody crapped out on me, thank God, so I had plenty of help."

"Did Charlotte show up?" Caution filled Sean's voice, which Conor didn't blame him for at all.

"She did and she worked like a dog." He couldn't fault his stepmother.

She'd arrived early on Friday after avoiding Thanksgiving dinner with her stepsons the day before, and had given her entire holiday weekend to pouring tastings and restocking racks. Conor had kept her up at the winery instead of letting her go down to work the tasting room in town. He wanted to watch and listen, see what she was saying to the townspeople and visitors to the winery. But Charlotte had been charming and circumspect, serving wine, telling the story of the Four Irish Brothers Winery with practiced panache, and accepting sympathy on the recent death of her husband and the brothers' father, Donal Flaherty, with a stoic smile.

"*She's* not our problem, Sean."

"I know. That's what Bren and Aidan keep saying." Sean's wariness came through loud and clear over the car speaker. "But she's allowing this, Con."

The four Flaherty brothers were currently involved in a legal tangle with their stepmother, who was contesting Donal's will, claiming she was owed part of the winery. But Conor and his brothers believed it was her two kids, not Charlotte, who wanted more of their father's estate, and either Charlotte was just too much of a wimp to fight them or they'd convinced her their claim was valid. Either way, it was a frustrating situation the four men had discussed endlessly from the first bite of turkey to the last bite of pie on Thanksgiving Day. They'd agreed earlier that one of Sean's associates from his Chicago law firm should take on the case, so he needed to get himself up to the winery and prepare for the meeting.

"What time are you meeting Sam?"

"In about an hour." Conor glanced at the car clock as he drove up the long driveway, passing row after row of vines.

"Call me when you're done?" Sean's tone softened. "It's going to be okay, man. She doesn't have a case."

"I know."

"Sam's been briefed and has all the documentation I have, but you'll need to provide the more personal details. Da's story of coming to America, buying the tobacco farm, and turning it into a winery. How hard he and Ma worked. You know—the family stuff we talked about this weekend." Conor pictured his brother leaning back in the big leather chair in his paneled office on the forty-seventh floor of a glass-and-steel skyscraper in Chicago.

"I know," Conor said again, and then feeling foolish, lied. "I've got the photos and journals ready. I'll call you, I promise."

He parked behind the huge barn that had housed Four Irish Brothers since his dad started the vineyard in 1976. Conor had heard the story from Da at least a thousand times—how he and his *darlin' Maggie* emigrated from Ireland the year of America's two-hundredth birthday, used their stash of savings to buy this old tobacco farm, and began planting grapes. Donal and Maggie had studied winemaking and learned all they could about the vines that the Swiss had brought to southern Indiana in the early nineteenth century. Maggie had worked in the business office of the barge shipyard down near the Ohio River while Donal renovated the barn and watched over the tender chambourcin, vignoles, and Riesling vines.

Life had been hard, but by the mid-eighties, Donal and Maggie had Four Irish Brothers Winery—named for their four sons—up and running. Ovarian cancer had stolen Maggie from them when Conor was in high school and now, Donal was gone, too. An aneurysm had dropped him in his tracks as he and Conor were barrel-tasting their first attempt at pinot noir, made from grapes they'd imported from a vineyard in Sonoma. The pinot was in the bottles now, four months later, and Brendan had come up with the name— Donal's Dream Pinot Noir—to honor Da.

Conor grimaced at the memory of catching his father in his arms that horrible summer day. If he thought about it very long, he could still hear Da's sudden intake of breath and the sound of the glass they'd shared shattering on the concrete floor of the cellar. Then his heart would ache at how much he'd lost in the past two years. So he didn't allow himself to think about it very often. Mostly, he set his grief aside to go about the business of being a single dad and a partner in a winery with his three brothers. But anger simmered in him since they'd received the letter from a Louisville attorney a couple of weeks ago—anger Conor wasn't sure he could tamp down like he had the grief. If Charlotte's greedy kids thought they were going to get their hands on Donal Flaherty's legacy, they were sadly mistaken.

"GOOD MORNING, MISS Hayes." Rose Gaynor's sunny smile greeted Sam as she entered the dining room of the Serendipity Inn.

The B&B definitely lived up to its hype on the web. Sam's room in the rambling Victorian was high-ceilinged, charming, and boasted an en suite bath, which was mandatory as far as Sam was concerned. She'd originally thought of booking at the chain hotel outside of town, but the Serendipity caught her eye on *Trip Advisor* as one of the top ten places to stay near River's Edge, Indiana. The pictures on their website reminded her of her aunt Bette's house in northern Indiana where Sam had spent nearly every summer of her childhood, so she'd booked the B&B instead.

She sniffed appreciatively. *Cinnamon, coffee, bacon—ahh.* "Good morning, Mrs. Gaynor. Everything smells heavenly."

The proprietor, who couldn't have been too much older than Sam herself, returned her smile. "Please, I'm just Rose. Help yourself to the buffet. Napkins and silverware are on the table. Sit anywhere. Can I pour you some juice or coffee?

Or do you prefer tea?"

"Coffee, please, with lots of half-and-half if you have it." Sam wandered over to the antique oak buffet covered with an array of amazing breakfast choices. "Oh, and call me Sam."

"Good morning, Sam." Rose grabbed a pot from the warmer while Sam filled a plate with fluffy scrambled eggs, a frosted cinnamon roll, a couple of slices of bacon and—surprise, surprise—fresh sliced tomatoes.

Sam settled into her chair and shook a gingham napkin into her lap. "I adore fresh tomatoes. These look delicious. Where did you find them at this time of year?"

"That's the last of the German pinks from my garden, I'm afraid." Rose sighed regretfully as she poured fragrant coffee into a sturdy mug and set it in front of Sam, along with a pottery mini-pitcher of cream. "I pick them green in late October and wrap them in brown tissue paper. Before you know it, red ripe tomatoes that are nearly as good as right from the vine."

"Have you been here long?" Sam was curious how such a young couple had managed to open a clearly successful B&B.

"We served our first guests five years ago. Tim and I found the old place when we were doing the Southern Indiana Wine Tour and fell in love immediately. So we sold everything we owned in Cincinnati and took the plunge. Tim's parents invested with us, but they stayed in Ohio."

"Was it in bad shape when you bought it?" Sam hoped

she wasn't prying, but curiosity made her press on.

"Not bad exactly, just needed some TLC and updating. We both love DIY, and I've always wanted to have a B&B. I got my degree in hospitality and tourism management at Purdue and had been working at a hotel in Cincy, and Tim worked for his dad's construction company. This was a good fit for both of us." She offered her own curious smile. "So, what brings you to River's Edge? We mostly serve couples, so having a single woman here is a little unusual."

"Just business in the area." Sam wasn't being deliberately obtuse. Professional ethics kept her from revealing what she was doing in the small river town. "But I hope I get to do some tourist things, too, while I'm here."

Rose set the coffeepot back on the warmer and returned to perch on a chair at Sam's table, something a server in Chicago wouldn't dare to do, but here, in this place, it was charming rather than disconcerting. "You missed Chautauqua—that was last month, but there's plenty to do yet—lots of fun shops and some good restaurants. Absolutely try Mac's Riverside Diner and taste some beer at The River Rat—great local microbrewery. Hutchin's House is the oldest continuously running restaurant on the Ohio River and Mario's has amazing pizza, although their lasagna is pretty great, too." She warmed to her subject, her love of her adopted home shining in her blue eyes. "The River Walk is loveliest in the spring and early fall, but it's a nice walk even this late in the season. Chilly, but pleasant. And we have several great wineries if you're a fan of wine. I've got some brochures in the lobby with lists and a map. I wish you could stay longer. In two weeks, we have the Christmas Candlelight Walk."

They chatted a bit more before a couple, clearly honeymooners, arrived and Rose hurried off to seat them. Sam almost reached for her phone to check her email, but changed her mind, deciding to enjoy the view of the Ohio River from the window next to her table. The morning sun cast peachy light across the water as a barge loaded with what looked like scrap metal chugged along. The trees had dropped nearly all their leaves, giving her an unobstructed view of the Kentucky hills across the river.

Although the scenery was amazing, Sam took up her phone and went through the checklist she'd made on in her *Notes* app, just to verify that she was more than prepared for her meeting with Sean's brother, Conor Flaherty. She'd read copiously for nearly three days, focusing on all the ins and outs of prenuptial agreements and wills and second marriages and property laws in the state of Indiana. Sean had given her copies of his father's prenup and will, the letter from the attorney in Louisville, and the involved document claiming that Donal's second wife had rights to more of his property than he'd left her in his will.

Sam wasn't worried; in spite of being married to Donal Flaherty for twelve years, the widow didn't have a case as far as Sam could see. His will appeared to be ironclad. Charlotte's argument was mainly based on her claim that Donal meant to change the terms, but died before he could do it. Without any evidence, that wouldn't hold up.

She took a deep breath and another sip of coffee, hoping against hope this case would never come before a judge. She hadn't been back in a courtroom since . . . she shivered. Not since that awful night . . .

In the few years since she'd joined the firm, she'd become the attorney of choice for wealthy women whose husbands had decided to turn them in for younger models. Most of the time, she didn't regret how ruthlessly she fought for the wives; those men got what they deserved. She also fought hard for women who were victims of spousal abuse. In those cases, her heart ached when the divorce also turned into a nasty custody battle; the last abuse case she'd worked on had been particularly brutal. In fact, it was the reason she was in River's Edge, helping the Flahertys.

The case had ended horribly one night when Carter Briggs, the abusive ex-husband, had gone on a rampage and shot his ex-wife, their three children, and himself in an hours-long siege with police. Sam had wept copious tears in Sean's office afterward, unable to fathom continuing her work there. He'd talked her down and assured her of the valuable part she played in women's lives, but somehow her heart was no longer in it. When she went to him a few weeks later to tell him she was thinking of leaving the firm, he'd rejected the idea immediately and instead asked her to come to the aid of his own family.

Shaking her head to dismiss the memory, she set the phone screen-side down on the table and concentrated instead on savoring every bite of breakfast, almost moaning aloud at the warm melt-in-her-mouth cinnamon roll. The delicious meal brought a moment of longing for childhood mornings in Aunt Bette's roomy kitchen, learning to make rolls and sipping café au lait as they waited anxiously while the bread baked. Mother was petite and very uptight, believing children should drink milk and water, nothing else, and that their diets should be strictly controlled—no sugar, no white flour, no caffeine, limited salt and fat. On the other hand, Aunt Bette was easygoing and believed food to be love, comfort, and pure pleasure. Sam definitely favored the Hayes side of her heritage. Her father, Judge Griffin Hayes, had been a lover of fine cuisine and wine and often took her to elegant restaurants as she was growing up, but he also enjoyed treks to little out-of-the-way places that served home cooking. His death when Sam was eighteen had left her bereft and her mother, Carlynne, even more closed up and distant. Dad would have loved this place. Mother would turn up her nose. Oh well, Sam would bring Aunt Bette down next time they decided to take one of their weekend road trips. Her dad's sister would be lyrical over Serendipity's cozy ambiance and delicious food.

Sam sipped her coffee and nibbled at the last of the cinnamon roll as she watched another barge out on the Ohio.

Mother missed out on so much by being rigid and not just about food, but pretty much about everything. She'd have been appalled at Rose's casual friendliness, as well as the informal buffet here at the B&B. Carlynne Hayes would have expected room service after waking up at five A.M. and taking a long brisk walk in the cold November morning. Not that Sam didn't respect a healthy exercise routine and keeping fit, she certainly did. She swam for exercise at the pool in the basement of her apartment building in Chicago and pretty much walked everywhere in the city, but unlike her mother, she allowed herself the pleasure of great food and wine, just as her dad had.

However, Sam was grateful for her mother's maternal loyalty and her unfailing pride in her daughter's career. Graduating near the top of her law school class at Northwestern had clinched Sam a spot in her mother's good graces for a long time to come, despite the fact that she'd chosen to go with a smaller firm in Chicago instead of the huge New York group her mother had been pushing for.

Sam glanced at her watch—an elegant wafer-thin Longines timepiece her mother had chosen for her as a graduation gift. It was beautiful, but Sam only wore it for work or when she went out to someplace fancy. Otherwise, she just checked her phone like everyone else she knew. It was only seven forty-five. She had time for a warm-up of Rose's amazing coffee before she headed out to Four Irish Brothers Winery and her meeting with Conor Flaherty.

Chapter Three

THE DRIVEWAY TO the Four Irish Brothers Winery wound through a hillside covered in vines and was narrow enough that Sam had to pull over onto the grass when a rickety flatbed truck heading out flew right past her. *Jerk.* He didn't even seem to notice her little car in the cloud of gravel dust he raised as he blew by. The scent of diesel fuel mixed with—*is that pine*—wafted after him. With an exasperated sigh, she straightened her wheel and got back onto the drive.

The vineyards on either side of the gravel were dormant now—the thick trunks of the plants extended mere skeleton-like vines that wrapped around wire and wood trellises. Several rows of plants were young—not even reaching the first row of wire supports. Perhaps they were experimenting with new varietals or just expanding their current grape choices. Right in the center of the vines sat a white filigree gazebo large enough to shelter at least twenty-five or thirty people. Several picnic tables were stacked up to one side, while beyond the vineyard, the still-green hills sloped into a wooded area that curtained her view of the Ohio below.

What a gorgeous setting! Donal and Maggie Flaherty had made the most of their location. The vineyards and stretches of verdant hills reminded Sam of a vacation to the Finger Lakes she'd taken with Aunt Bette a couple of years ago.

She caught her breath as she approached the cedar-and-glass structure that housed the tasting room and wine cellars. It was even more beautiful in person than it was on their website. Creeping into the parking area, she peered through the windshield, awed at how seamlessly Donal Flaherty had combined an old tobacco barn with the newer portion of the winery. Sort of Frank Lloyd Wright meets a Hoosier heartland farm, with a little Napa Valley tossed in for flavor.

As she climbed the steps to the wide deck, she realized what the flatbed had been doing there. A freshly cut Douglas fir, at least twelve feet tall, was leaning against the side of the building, while several boxes filled with pine roping and festive wreaths sat next to the stacked porch furniture. Apparently, he'd been delivering holiday decorations. She wandered closer to the wreath boxes. They were lovely. A couple of them were simply evergreen with pine cones and red plaid bows, another was holly with red berries and a white ribbon woven through the spiky leaves, but the largest one was a circle of fir branches bedecked with frosted pine cones and bunches of mistletoe tied with red-and-white ribbon.

Sam took a deep breath of piney deliciousness and was once again transported to Aunt Bette's cozy house and childhood Christmases. It was the one time a year that her mother actually relaxed just a little; the one time they were truly a family. The greenery summoned the heavenly scent of fresh sugar cookies and a Christmas tree. A fire crackling in the fireplace and five knit stockings hanging on the mantel. Her mother and Aunt Bette sipping mulled cider as they wrapped gifts at the dining room table, shooing her away if she happened in at the wrong moment.

A finger of cold air crept under her collar and Sam shivered back to the present. What was wrong with her? Ever since she'd come to River's Edge, she'd become downright nostalgic. But there was business to attend to here. She needed to stay in the present. A quick headshake later, she pinned on her no-nonsense attorney expression and reached for the knob on the wide paneled door to the tasting room.

The winery was dim and vast with a high beamed ceiling and a fieldstone fireplace that took up one entire end of the room. A round dark wood tasting bar stood in the middle, surrounded by several high-top tables and stools. One corner was the store with shelves of wine-themed tchotchkes of all kinds, while the back wall was nothing but racks and racks of bottles. A light shone from an office just to the right of the front door and plastic totes were piled haphazardly in front of an open closet nearby.

Sam cleared her throat. "Mr. Flaherty?" Her voice echoed slightly in the immense space.

She marched over to the office, her heels clicking loudly

29

on the hardwood floor. Nobody was there, although several photo albums and scrapbooks lay open on a rather cluttered desk. She glanced at her watch and then at a large wooden clock above the mantel. Nine on the dot. Obviously someone was here.

The door was unlocked; lights were on in the office. "Mr. Flaherty?"

"Oh, baby!" The deep voice came from somewhere below and she turned with a start, looking for the source.

"Excuse me?" She scanned the room, catching sight of a pair of double doors leading to a stairwell in the corner nearest to the office. Following sounds that could have been either ecstasy or pain, she descended the steps with trepidation.

"Oh, man." The voice became a moan.

"Um . . . Mr. Flaherty?" Sam reached the bottom of the stairs, a bit concerned at what she might encounter.

What if the guy down here was with a woman? On the other hand, what if he was hurt? She should probably investigate. She tiptoed timidly across the concrete floor.

"Oh, yes . . . yes!"

Okay, so he's not hurt.

Sam stopped dead in her track. "Excuse me?" she called into a room full of stainless-steel tanks, cases of wine, and stacked wooden barrels.

"Get in here!" the voice commanded, but this time it sounded familiar. "You have got to taste this." Heavy footsteps hurried toward her and around a tank appeared . . . *the man who had changed her tire yesterday?* He was holding a bottle in one hand and a small tumbler in the other, but practically squealed his tattered running shoes as he halted mid-step. "It's you."

They gazed at one another for a long moment, his blue eyes narrowing, color staining his cheeks. "Um, you want to try this? It's pretty amazing," he blurted as the flush on his face deepened from pink to scarlet.

She stepped back. "It's nine o'clock in the morning."

He eyed her, clearly debating what to say next. At last, he shrugged and the love of his product won out. "I know. But I wanted to taste it one more time before I put it up in the racks for sale." He held the wine up to the sunlight streaming in through the high window. "You can just spit it on the floor here if you want. I usually do but, man, this is too good not to swallow." He swished the wine around in the glass and extended it toward her.

Everything Sam knew about client meetings was suddenly upside down and, for a moment, she was at a loss. One didn't drink wine at a morning meeting or dress in jeans and a sweatshirt to meet their attorney. At least not in Chicago. She hesitated, meeting his blue, blue eyes over the tumbler and something in her released ever so slightly. Finally, she reached for the glass and offered a tentative smile.

With an abashed grin, he released the tumbler, talking a mile a minute as though he was really nervous. "It's my first attempt at Gewürztraminer. We harvested the first grapes from our north vineyard last fall. We had a cool summer last year, so they worked, which is remarkable since this isn't a grape that grows all that well here. Tell me what you think."

Sam accepted the wine, held the glass up to the light to admire the light-gold color before sniffing the aroma of citrus and apples, and then taking a sip. She swallowed simply because spitting in front of this delectable man was unthinkable.

"It's not actually sweet." She took another sip. "I always thought Gewürztraminers were sweet wines." Another sip and the tumbler was empty, leaving her feeling rather disappointed. "But this is light . . . delicious."

"What else?" His brown hair tumbled over his brow and even though he wasn't a particularly big man, he was taller than her—already a point in his favor. "What do you taste?"

"Apples? Like tart green apples and pineapple maybe"— she bit her lower lip—"citrus and something sweet, but not sugary. Honey?"

"Exactly!" He poured more wine into the short glass— not a wine stem, more like the kind of glass one would find wrapped in plastic in a hotel room. He nodded, his eyes sparking with excitement. "Try it again. It's *not* dessert, is it?"

Sam sipped and savored the crisp flavors of fruit and honey on her tongue. "No, it's for fish or cheese or summer evenings on the deck."

"You have a great palate." He took the glass, poured more wine and tasted, his eyes closed in obvious ecstasy, long sooty lashes resting on his cheeks.

His words of praise sent a not-unpleasant tingle down her spine. She couldn't remember ever seeing any man with such long, thick eyelashes . . . except for one—Sean Flaherty. "Are you Conor?" She met his gaze when he opened his eyes and then she knew for sure he had to be a Flaherty. They were as true cornflower blue as Sean's. Apparently, gorgeous ran in the family.

"I am. Conor Flaherty, winemaker extraordinaire at your service." He bowed with a cocky grin. "Would you like a job? I could use a cellar rat with a decent palate."

"I have a job." Sam returned the grin with a little swagger of her own. "I'm your attorney."

His eyes widened and his cheeks turned even redder. "*You're* Sam Hayes? Sean's law partner?" He set the glass on an upturned wooden barrel, wiped his fingers on his shirttail, and glanced at his watch before extending his hand. "Oh, damn, it's after nine."

She lingered over the handshake, enjoying his firm warm grasp, slightly sticky with wine. "I'm Samantha Hayes, Sean's *associate*."

He spread his fingers, palm up. "Sorry about that. You can wash your hands at that sink." He tilted his head toward a utility tub on the wall beside her. "There's soap and the towel's clean . . . mostly." Setting the bottle next to the tumbler on the barrel, he turned on the spigot.

Sam let warm water run over her fingers, moving over to allow Conor space at the sink. His shoulder, then his hip bumped hers chummily as they washed their hands together, and the tingle returned. Then each of them took an end of the white terry towel. As they dried their hands, for one inane moment, she was reminded of the dogs-sharing-spaghetti scene in the animated Disney movie *Lady and the Tramp* and she stifled a giggle.

Instead, she dropped her end of the towel and cleared her throat. From the moment she'd hit town, she'd been distracted by amazing pie, flat tires, a handsome samaritan, charming B&Bs, the wide restless river, and wine. Really, really good wine and a damn fine-looking winemaker. Time to focus on the business at hand. "Shall we go upstairs and talk about your situation?"

He gave her a wry smile and cocked his head toward the stairs. "Sure."

CONOR STEPPED BACK, allowing Samantha Hayes, attorney at law, to lead the way, aware that she was attempting to bring a more dignified tone to their meeting. But when she reached back, nabbed the open bottle of Gewürztraminer from the top of the barrel, and marched past him with it, he grinned. *Oh yeah, dignified. Very dignified.* And appealing, which surprised the hell out of him. After all, he hadn't so much as looked at another woman since Emmy.

Upstairs, he reached over the tasting bar, grabbed a couple of wine stems, and set them on one of the square hightop tables, grinning as her eyes widened. She was a dichotomy—snatching the wine bottle and bringing it up and then seeming surprised when he produced glasses. *Very interesting.* "Why don't we do this out here? My office is kind of a mess."

"Okay, that's fine." In spite of the slim skirt she wore, she hoisted herself up onto the stool he held out and opened her leather satchel.

He held up one finger. "I've got some things to show you—stuff Sean thought might help you build our case." He hustled into his office and collected up two photo albums and a scrapbook that contained pictorial records of Donal and Maggie Flaherty's journey from County Clare to a vineyard in southern Indiana. He added a pile of journals Donal had kept, in which he repeatedly wrote about the legacy he and Maggie would leave their sons.

When he glanced out at Sam, she was all business with a manila folder open in front of her and a legal pad set to one side. The bottle of Gewürztraminer she'd brought up from the cellar had been set aside, along with the two glasses as she sorted through a sheaf of papers in the folder. The woman was an enigma—a very attractive enigma to be sure. Again he was shocked at his level of interest, but now that he knew who she was, it was probably a bad idea to pour more wine. An intriguing notion, though . . . and she had brought the bottle up.

Sean might have warned him that Sam Hayes was a woman, but it probably hadn't even occurred to him to mention it. To Sean, she was simply an associate in his firm, not a potential mate for his widowed younger brother.

His brothers understood the depth of the pain he'd suffered during Emmy's illness and death. And although they worried about him living like a virtual monk, neither Sean nor Bren nor Aidan had suggested Conor begin dating again, at least not yet. Certainly the three of them had talked about his grief—they wouldn't be Flahertys if they weren't discussing among themselves ways to help him. It was how their family had always worked, but they hadn't staged an intervention yet. Unless . . . *could* Sam Hayes be Sean's attempt to bring his brother out of the darkness?

He eyed her from the doorway of his office. Her abundant auburn hair was carefully pulled back into a tidy knot at the nape of her neck, but he recalled clearly the cloud of curls that had escaped her hood when he changed her tire in the rain. And the brown eyes that shone with humor and compassion even in the frustration of car trouble on a drizzly November Sunday; he definitely remembered *them*. Now she sat with her back to him, her slender shoulders stiff, long shapely legs crossed at the ankles as her feet rested on the rung of the stool. Not many women could pull off elegant perched on a barstool, but Sam was managing quite nicely.

"Did you find a place to get your tire fixed?" Conor placed the albums, scrapbooks, and journals on the table as he slid onto the stool opposite Sam.

"Not yet. I'm still driving on the spare." She pulled out what appeared to be a very expensive pen. "Can you recommend a place around here or do I need to go to Cincinnati? After I drove through Indianapolis, I didn't see much in the way of big cities."

"There's a tire store up at the top of the hill." He pointed, and at her furrowed brow, realized she probably wouldn't know the locals' term for the stretch of highway above River's Edge. One could find nearly anything there from chain restaurants and gas stations to a Target, a Kroger, and even a Starbucks. "Up on the highway, there are all kinds of businesses, including a couple of tire stores. I can call Big O and see if they can get it taken care of for you, if you like."

"Thanks, I appreciate it, but I can call them." She chuckled and his belly tightened.

Her voice made him think of zin or petit Syrah—sultry and husky and as captivating as wine and chocolate. As a matter of fact, everything about her made him hungry, and that was something entirely new and unexpected, too. Since Emmy's death, most food had tasted like ashes. He cooked for Ali and he ate because it was important to keep his strength up, but there was no pleasure in it anymore. Suddenly, as he eyed the new Gewürztraminer, he longed for apples and cheese and a loaf of warm crusty French bread. He eyed her for a moment before pushing away from the table. "Let's have some more wine and we need something to eat with it."

Again she stared at him in disbelief. "It's nine o'clock in the morning."

"So?"

When she shook her head, a wisp of russet curl released to curve across her cheek. "I ate breakfast, thanks."

"I didn't. Think of it as brunch. People drink mimosas in the morning all the time." Conor had no idea why it was so important to share food with this woman, but he found apples and an unopened chunk of Port Salut cheese in the chiller under the tasting bar and brought them to the table along with a paper plate and two small paring knives. He snatched the last loaf of bread from the display rack that Paula Meadows kept full from her bakery in town. It was probably still fresh enough. He wanted to watch Samantha Hayes eat, to see if she brought as much enjoyment to food as she did to the wine.

She was clearly struggling with the idea of their meeting turning into brunch, but when he set the food on the table, she reached for the cheese, turning it over in her hands. "Is that Port Salut?" Her fingers were long, her wrists delicate, and her nails neatly manicured with a hint of pale polish. "I love this cheese and it's hard to find."

He grinned. *I knew it!* She would be eating with him and

that brought a moment of surprising delight. She was a foodie. Conor had been one, too, before Emmy's death had left him bereft and unable to enjoy the taste of anything, even the delicious turkey dinner Aidan and Sean had collaborated on for Thanksgiving. Bren had brought his favorite half-moon cookies from Baltimore, but Conor had barely tasted one. He wished the box was here instead of back at the house. His stomach was growling as he watched Sam unwrap the cheese, noticing again her short, perfect nails.

He hated long, brightly painted fingernails, although red toenails were one of his turn-ons. Emmy always had plain fingers and hot crimson toes—one of the sexy quirks he'd fallen in love with back when they'd started dating in junior high school. Pedicures had always been what she called her "Zen time," and when she'd become too ill to leave the house, Conor had massaged her feet with lotion each night to help her relax.

He shook his head to clear it and stopped short of speculating whether Sam's toes matched her conservative manicure, instead wondering again if Sean had sent her down to River's Edge for more than legal advice. He could've sent anyone from his firm, but it would be just like him to toss a pebble into the deep water of Conor's sorrow by sending someone like Sam Hayes.

Chapter Four

S AM UNWRAPPED THE cheese and set it on the plate as Conor opened the bread and sliced one of the apples. For some unfathomable reason, she was starving, even after having just finished breakfast at Serendipity an hour earlier. And wine at nine thirty in the morning? *Seriously?*

Everything about this morning was wrong, but somehow, it suddenly felt very right as Conor laid apple slices on a paper plate and tore open the bread. So she picked up the other paring knife and added pieces of cheese to the feast.

She nibbled a stray sliver. "This Port Salut is delicious."

"We get our cheeses from a dairy over near Cincy— Sycamore Hills. They have an amazing operation—it's huge. They even do tours of the facility. I took Ali over to see a baby calf being born a couple of months ago and . . . Well, anyway. They make good cheese . . . and ice cream." Dull red flushed his cheeks again, his embarrassment painfully obvious.

He was rambling; something Sam did herself when she was nervous. How funny that *she* was making *him* nervous. The whole morning had turned into something entirely different than what she had prepared for, and it was becoming harder and harder to maintain her attorney face.

She smiled, hoping to ease his discomfort. "Ali?" She quirked one brow. "Your daughter? The one in the car yesterday?"

"Yes." He didn't meet her gaze. Instead he focused on the apple, cutting it into precise sections. "She's four."

"And your wife? Does she help in the winery?"

He gave her a hard stare. "My wife is dead. Sean didn't tell you?"

Now she was the one blushing. "I'm so sorry. No, he didn't mention that when he prepared me to speak to you about the case." *Damn you, Sean. Thanks a lot.* "May I ask what happened?"

"Pancreatic cancer." Sadness fell like a veil over his eyes and the sparkle disappeared. "When Ali was two."

A wave of pity washed over Sam, but she was pretty sure she didn't need to show that to Conor. Instead she handed him a paper plate and reached for the bread. "Is this from a local bakery? I don't recognize the brand." She held the brown paper package up to read the label.

"Paula Meadows has Bread & Butter in town." His tone brightened as he gave her a grateful smile. "Best bakery on the river. Her doughnuts are gone by ten every morning, so you have to get there early. And, man, her challah is amazing. This nine grain is Ali's favorite."

Sam set a piece of cheese on the rich dark bread, took a

bite, and almost moaned. She closed her eyes, savoring the nutty flavor in combination with the rich smooth cheese.

When she opened them, Conor's grin lit up his face. "You're a foodie." It wasn't an accusation, simply a statement of fact. He poured wine into the glasses and handed her one.

"I am," she admitted and, after a moment's hesitation, accepted the glass and took a sip of wine. Obviously this business meeting was taking a different track, but then Conor Flaherty wasn't the client she'd expected either. She allowed the wine to relax her—the tension in her shoulders releasing as she settled into her chair. "Although, except for mimosas, I don't think I've ever had wine this early in the morning before. My dad was a gourmet. He taught me to love good food."

"Ah, then you'll have to be sure to hit Mac's Riverside Diner in town while you're here." Conor sandwiched a couple of slices of apple and one of cheese between two pieces of bread.

"Diner food was one of Dad's favorite things. He'd have lost his mind over Millie's chicken and dumplings."

He nodded, obviously familiar with the little pie emporium several miles north. "Oh, Millie's is great, but Mac's isn't your usual diner fare, even though he does great biscuits and gravy, and his pork cutlets are worth the trip to town on Thursday nights." Conor took a quick sip of wine. "Mac Mackenzie is a Le Cordon Bleu chef. Trained in Paris and worked at Le Café Tournon before he came back home and opened the Riverside with his daughter, Megan."

Sam nearly choked on a bite of apple. "A Le Cordon Bleu chef owns the local diner?" This town was becoming more fascinating every moment, and not just because Conor Flaherty's French accent was impeccable.

"Yup. His menu includes something unusual every week—last week I heard it was pumpkin and prawn risotto." Her eyes must have been huge because Conor chuckled. "Dunno what's coming up this week, but I imagine it'll be something with turkey because he cooks about five huge ones for the orphan's Thanksgiving that he hosts every year."

"Orphan's Thanksgiving?"

"Anyone who doesn't have family in the area or a place to go on Thanksgiving is welcome at the diner for a free meal. He and Megan serve about fifty or so every year. His brined turkey and oyster dressing are famous up and down the river." He popped another bite of cheese into his mouth, clearly savoring the creamy taste.

"What a nice thing for him to do." Sam thought about her own quiet Thanksgiving dinner at her mother's elegant apartment on Lakeshore Drive. The two of them shared appropriately sized servings of roasted turkey, baked sweet potatoes, asparagus, and salad with oil and vinegar at a mahogany dining table that could've seated ten more people quite comfortably. A brisk walk along the lakeshore was followed by a small piece of rather nondescript pumpkin pie and decaf because caffeine after four in the afternoon was verboten.

Sam had been back at her own small apartment near Printer's Row by six, tossing off her heels and beige sheath and pulling on yoga pants and a fraying Northwestern sweatshirt. She spent Thanksgiving night alone, devouring a huge slice of Hoosier Mama pumpkin pie slathered with whipped cream, washed down with apple cider and cinnamon schnapps as she wept over *It's a Wonderful Life*. And missed her father so much she could hardly breathe.

"River's Edge is a pretty great town." Pride filled Conor's tone and shone in his blue eyes.

Sam was struck again at his resemblance to Sean, whom she'd always had a little bit of a crush on ever since she'd started at the firm six years ago. Both men were well-built and had thick chestnut-colored hair and the bluest eyes she'd ever seen, although Conor could use a few more pounds on his six-foot or so frame. He wasn't thin, just slightly less brawny than Sean, and she wondered if he'd lost weight when his wife was sick. She smiled to herself as she watched him devour more bread and cheese. There was certainly nothing wrong with his appetite today.

She set aside her plate and wineglass and glanced down at the folder before her. It was time to bring this meeting back around to its true purpose. After all, the lawsuit was why she was here. "There are four of you, right? And you're all in agreement about this suit?"

From gossip among the other associates and support staff

around the firm, she knew a little something about at least one of Conor's other brothers—the actor Aidan Flaherty. He played a cop on a popular TV show that Sam had only seen once after she learned about the connection. She wasn't into TV crime dramas all that much. She'd seen him in person, though. Several of the paralegals had swooned and giggled last year when he'd shown up at the office one day to go to lunch with Sean. Aidan was also quite handsome, but blond and not as tall or broad as his brothers. She remembered he'd signed some autographs in the hallway outside the break room. The other brother, Brendan, was some sort of government type and lived in Washington, DC. She couldn't help but wonder if he was brown-haired and strapping like Conor and Sean or blond and lithe like Aidan.

"Yes." When Conor swallowed and nodded, his hair flopped onto his forehead, and she knit her fingers together, fighting an urge to brush it back in place.

He needed a haircut. Thick brown waves crept over the collar of his chambray shirt and curved around his ears. It was distracting and merely sitting across from him sent a little zing through her veins that seemed very unprofessional. Picking up her pen, she focused on the paperwork. "All four of you?"

"We're all in this together; we agree that we have to fight her." He nodded, taking another sip of wine. "Charlotte is a good woman. I like her. She and Da seemed pretty happy together, which is why her contesting his will was such a shock. It was never his intention that she have any stake in the winery and she knows that." He glanced around the vast space and sighed. "Sean's not convinced and neither is Aidan, but Bren and I are sure it's her kids that are behind this."

She met his eyes across the table. "Tell me why."

SAMANTHA HAYES WAS suddenly all business as she un-capped her pen and gazed at him over the remains of the food. It was as if she'd flipped a switch—and the meeting turned back into one between an attorney and her client instead of . . . Well, Conor had to confess that sitting with her at the pub table, sharing food and wine, and chatting had almost felt like a first date. Which was just stupid. Sam was here to help him fight this lawsuit. Nothing more.

But that didn't change the fact she'd been on his mind since he'd first seen her, rain-drenched and frustrated on the side of Drury Road the day before. Or that she was the only woman to pique his interest since Emmy had caught his eye outside the band room in eighth grade. Most especially, she was the only woman to make him hungry for things he hadn't had an appetite for in two years. He was surprised that even after eating three pieces of bread, nearly the entire apple, and most of the cheese she'd sliced, his mind was wandering to leftover pie and turkey and Mac's amazing eggs

Benedict . . . and Samantha Hayes's plump pink lips.

Those lips remained in a straight line as she asked him leading questions about Charlotte's son and daughter, whom he believed lived in mortal fear of having to be responsible for their aging mother.

"I . . . *we,* really, think," he insisted, "that they're just trying to make sure she doesn't end up on one of their doorsteps."

Sam's brow furrowed. "According to the information Sean gave me, she's well-provided for—long-term care insurance that will be paid until she dies, a tidy cash inheritance, and you've said she's welcome to live in the house that she and your dad shared here on the property. Plus, from what I could dig up on her financials, she came into the marriage pretty comfortable anyway—from the death of her first husband."

"Yeah, that's always been my understanding. He was president of his family's bank across the river in Kentucky. She and Da met when she and some friends came to a pizza-and-wine night a few years after our mother passed. She's a lovely lady, and Da had been alone for a long time. We were happy for him."

"So no wicked stepmother stories for me?" Her expression was serious in spite of her teasing words.

"None." Conor shook his head as he wrapped up the cheese and scraped the paring knife against the edge of a paper plate. "Her kids have never impressed me, though—

the daughter, Sabrina, reminds me of those dizzy debutantes from the sixties, and Rob had a job in his dad's bank, but frankly, he's just a lazy bum now. They never come to see her. She's always the one who goes to visit them. At least that was the case until Da died. Now, they're playing the concerned children role ad nauseam."

Sam flipped through some papers. "You're certain your dad never mentioned leaving her any interest in Four Irish Brothers? She says in her statement that he promised she'd be one-fifth owner upon his death, but that he hadn't had time to change his will when he passed."

"That's complete crap." His harsh words echoed in the high-ceilinged room and heat rose to his cheeks. "Sorry. This whole thing just makes me furious. We hadn't even had time to grieve before she . . . *they* hit us."

"I understand." Sam gave him a sympathetic smile as he dumped the vestiges of their impromptu meal in the trash can under the tasting bar and recorked the bottle of Gewürztraminer. "It's our job to prove her wrong."

Conor grabbed a bar towel and swiped at the bread crumbs on the table. The whole situation with Charlotte made his stomach knot. The winery had always held its own, without Sean or Brendan or Aidan having to pitch in any of their own hard-earned money. It was a point of pride for Conor to keep it that way. If she won this contest and they ended up having to buy her out, he'd have to accept money from Aidan to purchase new fermentation tanks and the desperately needed French oak casks he and Da had been eyeing before Da had died. Renovating and expanding the gazebo would have to wait at least another year or two. Plus the riverside tasting room down in town needed a new roof. Paying off Charlotte would take a healthy chunk out of the winery's budget.

The money wasn't the only issue. Charlotte was the only grandmother Ali knew since Emmy's parents lived in California now. The kid adored her Grammy Char. The suit had already caused an uncomfortable rift between him and his stepmother, and Ali was bound to pick up on the tension. He had to fight the contest, but he sensed Charlotte wouldn't stick around if she lost and the thought sobered him. If it was only her, he and his brothers might've just cut her into the winery, but that wasn't the case. Her will left everything to her two children and the last thing in the world Conor wanted was to have Sabrina and Rob under his skin for the rest of his natural life.

No, fighting was the right thing.

With a sigh, he handed the stack of journals to Sam. "Here are a few of Da's journals. He kept one every year of his life as far as I know. I pulled the ones from the year he and Ma opened the winery, the year Ma died, the year he met and married Charlotte, and the last two years. And a couple of other random ones, just so you can see how . . . how *passionate* he was about leaving the place to us." He opened a worn black marbled composition notebook and flipped through the pages before setting it in front of her. "See? He named it Four Irish Brothers because of us and that was back when we were little kids. They opened when Aidan was barely a year old." He paced, too tense to sit still.

Sam read the scrawled words silently, turning the page, reading, then turning it again. Conor wasn't sure how fascinating Da's life was to a big-city attorney, but he wanted her to know how important it had been to Donal Flaherty that his sons own the winery that was his life's work. Apparently, he'd misjudged her level of interest because she read for several minutes, going back to the beginning pages of the first journal, studying Da's words intently.

Suddenly, she shut the journal and stood up. "I want to meet her."

"You mean now?" He glanced at his watch, surprised to see that over two hours had passed since Sam had arrived. No doubt Charlotte would be up at the house preparing her lunch.

"No." She chewed her lower lip thoughtfully. "Is there a way I can meet her without her knowing who I am or why I'm here? Can we invent some social situation?"

From the gleam in her brown eyes, she was plotting something. He couldn't imagine what, but he was game if it meant keeping his winery safe. Surprising himself, he offered impulsively, "Tonight's our tree-trimming. Char always helps decorate the winery on the Monday after Thanksgiving. I assume she'll be here. It's an event we don't have to create. Friends from town come up. Why don't you join us?"

She smiled a mysterious little smile and started gathering up the journals. "Perfect. I'd love to come. Can you make sure she's here?"

"Yeah, I'll stop by the house and remind her that Ali will want her to help." He paused, unsure how to continue. "If we don't tell her who you are, why you're here, she's going to make assumptions." He flushed with heat, too aware that a red blush was spreading up his neck and into his face. "I mean . . . you know . . . she'll think that you're . . . that we . . ."

What was it about this woman that made him as comfortable as an old friend one moment and as tongue-tied as a middle-school kid the next? The feelings were way different from the numbness he'd felt for the last two years, but he was pretty sure he wanted to explore the phenomenon further and that surprised him even more.

"She can think whatever she wants. As a matter of fact, if she thinks we're . . ." Now she was red-faced, but she shook her head as if to clear it. "If she thinks we're dating, she'll be relaxed and maybe she'll talk to me."

"Are you thinking you can talk her out of this?" Conor had serious doubts. He and his brothers had all taken a shot trying to convince Charlotte to drop the suit. Although she seemed sad about suing them, she was determined to go through with it. "Don't count on it."

"I just want to meet her. See who she is." Sam shoved her

notebook and file folder into her bag and pointed to the journals. "May I take these with me? I want to read through them this afternoon. I'll keep them safe, I promise, and bring them back to you tomorrow."

"Of course. Keep them as long as you need to."

"What time tonight?"

"Six?" Conor reviewed the contents of his pantry in his head as he spoke, trying to remember if he had everything he needed for the potato-leek soup he made every year or whether he'd have to make a trip up the hill. "It's supper— we have soup and bread while we decorate. Tradition."

"Can I bring something?" Sam slipped into her coat and buttoned it before wrapping a soft scarf around her throat and tugging on a pair of leather gloves. "Why don't I go by that bakery in town and pick up dessert?"

"Sure." A shiver of excitement eddied through him as she strode to the door.

Hand on the knob, she turned and asked the one question guaranteed to win his heart, though he was certain she had no way of knowing that. "What would Ali like?"

Chapter Five

"CAN I BRING you a cup of tea or hot chocolate?" Rose Gaynor's voice brought Sam back to the cozy living room of the B&B, where she was curled up in a wing chair by the fire reading Donal Flaherty's journals.

"I'd love a hot chocolate. Thank you, Rose." When Sam stretched her arms above her head and yawned, the notebook she'd been so wrapped up in slid from her lap. She rescued it before it hit the floor and smoothed the paper before closing the worn pages.

A quick glance at the mantel clock told her she'd been sitting for the better part of three hours, but she'd been so enraptured by the journals, she'd barely noticed the shadows lengthening across the patterned rug. Her plan had been to skim through the diaries that Conor had given her, looking for quotes that related to Donal's desire to leave the winery to his sons, and she had noted several. However, his writing was so lyrical and his storytelling so captivating; she'd gone back to the beginning and read every sentence. Somehow it seemed as if she could hear his thick Irish brogue in those written words.

"Must be some pretty fascinating stuff," Rose observed, one eyebrow quirked.

"Just some research," Sam downplayed. Professional ethics prevented her from expanding, so she gave Rose a smile as she tucked the journal into her bag with the others. "I need to stand up and move. Let me run this up to my room and then I'll help you with the cocoa."

"It's warming on the stove." Rose returned the smile, curiosity still evident in her gray eyes. "Just come down to the kitchen when you're ready." She turned, but Sam stopped her with a hand on her arm.

"Do you know what time the bakery in town closes?"

"Paula's open 'til six." Rose hesitated in the doorway. "If you're looking for a treat, I have some of her cookies to go with your hot chocolate."

"Thank you, but I want to get something for"—Sam paused, figuring she might as well go ahead and keep as close to the truth as she could—"for a tree-trimming party I've been invited to up at Four Irish Brothers Winery."

Rose's eyebrow lifted again and her eyes widened in surprise. "You know the Flahertys?"

Vacillating between revealing her true reason for being in River's Edge and keeping it a secret from Charlotte Flaherty and her kids, Sam simply nodded. "Yes."

When Sam didn't offer any more details, Rose cocked her head toward the kitchen. "You'll have time for a cup of hot chocolate before you go to the bakery. It's just a few blocks up, at the corner of Spruce and Main."

Back in her room, Sam glanced in the mirror above the dresser. The comfortable yoga pants and sweatshirt she changed into earlier wouldn't do for the party, although the suit she'd worn that morning wasn't appropriate, either. She yanked open the wardrobe, wondering what was appropriate for a tree-trimming at a small-town winery. After a moment's perusal, she selected a pair of elegant slacks and a cream silk blouse. She could pair her long red cardigan and her black boots with the outfit for a more casual holiday look. Thank heaven it had occurred to her to pack something other than yoga pants and her suits, but now she wished she'd packed a pair of jeans.

Pulling out the hairpins she'd placed so carefully, she shook her head and ran her fingers through her hair before she flipped on the light in the roomy bath. Rose's impeccable taste showed throughout the whole B&B, but her woman's touch was obvious in the bathroom, where the lighting was perfect for applying makeup and the tub was deep and inviting. Votive candles lined up on the wide surround, along with several kinds of bath salts and a basket of soaps. She gazed at the bath longingly, turning away when the mantel clock chiming four strokes reminded her she didn't have time. She'd save the soak for when she got back tonight.

Instead, she washed her face, redid her makeup, applying a smoky shadow that made her brown eyes appear even larger, and pulled her hair up into a messy bun. Tendrils of hair curled over her cheeks and down her neck. A hint of glossy color on her lips and she was ready to play the part of Conor Flaherty's new "friend." She clutched for a moment. They needed a story about who she was and why Charlotte had never met her before.

Dressing quickly, she grabbed her phone and thumbed a quick text to Conor. *"What's our story?"*

His answer came back so fast it startled her. *"I've been thinking about that."*

"OK."

"How about we say we met through Sean? The closer we stick to the truth, the better, don't you think?"

Sam grinned. Look at that. A man who punctuated text messages and used real words and complete sentences, not those idiotic acronyms and emojis that drove her so nuts. *How refreshing!* She'd stopped dating a guy who worked at the stock brokerage on the floor below the law firm because he never used a comma or a period in a text and sent her too-cute little animal emojis while she was working. Well, that wasn't the whole reason, but if she was honest, it certainly played into her decision to end the relationship after four dates.

"That sounds good. I'll follow your lead," she returned.

"Great. See you soon."

Sam held her breath. That was it. No smiley face. No cutesie-pie bunny or snowman or Santa. The man used texting for the utility of quick communication and not to flirt or try to disarm her. Conor Flaherty was becoming more appealing by the minute and that both delighted and dismayed her.

She bit her lower lip as her fingers hovered over her phone. How tempting it was to call Aunt Bette to process through this roller coaster of feelings she'd been experiencing since her arrival in River's Edge. The rush of nostalgia, the fear and longing, and an attraction so strong she wanted to hurtle herself into a certain winemaker's arms had her seriously considering packing up and heading straight back to Chicago. This trip was not turning out to be what she'd planned at all.

Magically, the phone vibrated in her hand. *Aunt Bette.* Honestly, the woman was psychic. Sam dashed one finger across the screen as she perched on the edge of the wing chair by the window. "Aunt Bette! I was just thinking of you."

Her aunt's chuckle warmed her right down to her socks. "I guess we must have been getting each other's vibes, kid. You've been on my mind all day. How ya doin'? How'd your meeting go?"

"It was good." Sam took a deep breath. "Better than good. I'm pretty sure I can win this case with no problem. Actually, I'm kinda hoping it'll never get to a courtroom."

"That's great, honey." Bette paused and when Sam didn't continue, her voice deepened with worry. "Do I hear a *but* coming? What's up? Is this guy a jerk?"

Sam laughed, grateful for Bette's down-to-earth concern. Suddenly her attraction to Conor seemed less daunting. "No, he's not at all. Quite the opposite actually. As a matter of fact, turns out he's the samaritan who rescued me on the road yesterday afternoon."

"So that really was an honest-to-God meet-cute?"

Heat crept up Sam's neck and she was grateful they weren't on FaceTime or Bette would've noticed immediately. "You old romantic! He's a client, Aunt Bette, and I just met him. So don't start matchmaking."

"I'm not," Bette denied. "I can tell from your voice you're attracted to this man, though."

"Oh, I don't know." Sam sighed. "Okay, I am, but he's my boss's brother, and I'm also fairly sure there's something unethical about wanting to jump your client's bones."

"Good heavens, girl, this is a whole new you. The attorney I know would never even consider mixing business with pleasure."

Sam could picture Bette's perfectly arched brows pinched together in a frown. Some people might think it weird that her best friend was also her aunt, but Bette Hayes had been her big sister, her playmate, her confidant, and her best friend since she'd spent her first summer in Aunt Bette's cottage near the dunes in northern Indiana. Sam was six that summer and twenty-seven-year-old Bette had just published her first novel—a middle-grade mystery with a thirteen-year-old hero named Timothy Titus. The book took off and over the years Bette had written an entire series of Timothy Titus stories, taking the young detective on adventures across the country.

Summers with Aunt Bette were the best times of Sam's

childhood, and later, in her teen and college years, she traveled with Bette all over North America to find new settings for the Timothy books. Her dad's sister loved life and food and adventure and was just the opposite of Sam's tightly wound mother. And although it had bothered her a little that her mother released her to Bette's care every summer without so much as a backward wave, Sam wouldn't have dreamed of asking to stay in Chicago during her school breaks. Bette and Sam grew as close as sisters while the gap between Sam and her mother widened with each passing summer.

"I'm not." Sam dropped back into the chair with a sigh. "Truly. It's just . . ."

"Just what? Kiddo, you're ripe for a love affair. After all, it's been over a year since you broke up with that schmuck your mother was so fond of. David Walter Grant III." Bette's tone turned chilly as she intoned the name of the man Sam had dated all through law school and for several years after.

"He broke up with me."

"Po-tay-to, po-tah-to." Sam could picture her aunt's careless shrug. "Same result, thank God."

Sam had come dangerously close to marrying David Grant before she realized something vital was missing from their relationship. She wasn't sure at the time what it was, but when he kept pushing her for a wedding date, she couldn't commit.

When the ultimatum finally came one sweltering August

night and he demanded she set a date, she'd simply stared at him. With a firm, "Okay then, we're done," he'd shaken his head, held his hand out for the pricey ring that she'd worn for three years, and muttered something about wasting too many years waiting for her to make a decision. The ring slipped off too easily and he left her standing alone on the sidewalk outside the Chicago Stock Exchange. Rather than wallowing in the melancholy that should have happened because her fiancé of three years had just kicked her to the curb, Sam had grabbed a cab and gone down to skip barefoot along the shore of Lake Michigan, basking in cool water, silvery moonlight, and blessed freedom.

Not wanting to fall into the quicksand of that particular topic, she straightened and gave a short laugh. "Be that as it may, dear Bette, that's not what's going on here. Not with a client and certainly not with Sean Flaherty's brother."

"Then what *is* going on?" Her aunt was relentless when it came to Sam's well-being.

"I think the holidays are making me sappy and sad," Sam dissembled. "Thanksgiving sorta sucked, and you know how much I miss Dad around the holidays. Plus, this town is almost too charming and—"

"And the winemaker is a hottie," Bette put in with a chuckle.

"And the winemaker is a hottie," Sam agreed, grateful for the levity that had crept into the conversation. "Hot or not, though, he's a client, so that's that." Quickly, she switched topics. "You'd love this little town. It's adorable. I almost wish I could stay longer and see it all dressed up for Christmas."

They chatted for a few more minutes before Bette had to sign off. "Keep me posted, Sammi." Her aunt's use of Sam's old nickname brought a lump to her throat.

Swallowing hard, she managed a breezy good-bye and, with one more peek in the mirror, gathered up her coat, knitted scarf, and purse and headed out the door, ready for Rose's cocoa and later, what just might prove to be a very interesting evening.

SAM DREW IN a breath at the sight of the winery transformed with white Christmas lights and fresh garland. The pine trees around the deck twinkled invitingly in the dusk and two of the wreaths she'd seen earlier hung on the double doors. Someone had been busy. Hot chocolate and cookies in Rose's roomy old-fashioned kitchen had put her in the holiday spirit and the brisk walk to Bread and Butter sent another wave of nostalgia skimming through her. Folks were stringing white twinkle lights from streetlight to streetlight across Main Street, while others wrapped lampposts in green garland. River's Edge was turning into a Christmas fairyland.

A few cars were in the parking lot, and the sight of two golf carts shrouded in heavy clear plastic enclosures brought a smile to her lips. Who knew someone could make a golf cart weatherproof? Her little car fit nicely between a huge pickup and a battered Jeep, and Sam ran around to the passenger's side to collect her purse and the neatly tied gingham box from the Bread and Butter bakery.

A tinge of anticipation shivered through her at the thought of opening the box for Conor's daughter. He'd mentioned that Ali liked cupcakes and Paula Meadows had a delicious assortment of flavors to choose from, including key lime, which had made Sam's mouth water. There was a pink one with strawberry icing and a candy snowman perched on top that she'd chosen especially for the little girl.

Low lights along the parking lot led her right to the steps of the deck and the sound of holiday music and laughter drifted out through the heavy oak doors. Warm light glowed in the windows and she resisted the urge to peer inside. Instead she paused for a moment, straightened her shoulders both literally and figuratively and, balancing the box on one arm, she stepped inside.

The heavy door bumped shut behind her and the chatter in the room stopped as Conor Flaherty, looking handsomer than ever in jeans and a plaid flannel shirt, looked up and released the tangle of what appeared to be wine corks strung on wire back into the box at his feet.

"Sam!" With a smile that sent her heart thumping, he hurried over to relieve her of the box as he dropped a quick kiss on her cheek. "Glad you made it."

Chapter Six

CONOR HOPED HIS body hid the stunned expression on her face from the rest of the people gathered around the stone fireplace, although he was certain that particular look was mirrored on their faces as well. The gesture had been meant to put her at her ease. She'd come in huge-eyed, more like a cornered rabbit than the confident attorney who'd strode out earlier that day. He'd been damn nervous himself all afternoon as he'd wound twinkle lights around the outside trees and draped pine garland along the deck rail. So much so that even Nate noticed when he'd reported for work after school and kidded him about being all thumbs.

"I'm way overdressed," she murmured as he pulled back to help her off with her coat.

"You're perfect." He assured her in a hasty whisper, and she was.

The rich red sweater brought out auburn lights in the tendrils of hair that had escaped her bun and curled on her neck while the fashionable high-heeled boots put her luscious lips nearly on a level with his. That particular temptation sent a shiver of anticipation through him.

Sam recovered her poise quickly enough though, as she yanked off her gloves, shrugged out of her camel-hair coat, and handed it to him along with her bright scarf. He hung it on a row of pegs near the office and with a hand on her lower back, led her to the group staring openly at the two of them. "Everyone, this is Sam Hayes." He stretched out an arm. "Sam, everyone."

His circle of friends opened then and Meg stepped forward, her blonde hair gleaming in the lights. "Hi, Sam, I'm Megan Mackenzie." She extended her hand as Conor tossed her a grateful smile.

"Meg's our mayor, as well as one of the owners of Mac's Riverside Diner." Conor grasped Sam's elbow in a gesture he hoped would be perceived as proprietary.

"Hello, Megan. Your dad's the gourmet chef?" Sam shook hands firmly while at the same time giving Conor an over-the-shoulder smile so warm it sent heat sizzling through his veins.

Oh yeah, she's going to play along.

"Conor's told me I have to catch supper at your restaurant while I'm here. What's the special this week?"

Megan chuckled. "Dad's down at the diner right now doing mysterious and wonderful things with leftover turkey. Do stop by. Whatever it is, you don't want to miss it."

"And this is Tierney Ashton." Conor kept Sam close to his side as he moved around the circle. "She's not only the assistant chief of our fire department and our head paramedic, she's also the local crop duster."

"I even take tourists on helicopter rides over the river during the county fair every summer." Tierney's wide grin and pixie freckles had disarmed Conor ever since they'd shared a seat on the bus way back in elementary school and she didn't fail him now. She greeted Sam with a friendly hug. "So glad to meet you, Sam."

"Here are her mom, Teresa, who's president of the River's Edge Bank, and Frank, her dad, who's our fire chief."

Frank and Teresa greeted Sam with enthusiasm and unabashed curiosity as Conor quickly introduced the rest of his guests.

"This is Nate, the skate, Tierney's nephew—"

"Chief cellar rat at your service." Tall as his aunt was tiny, lanky sixteen-year-old Nathan Ashton grinned and nudged Conor with a wink as he nodded to Sam.

"Nice to meet you, Nate." Sam returned the boy's greeting. "I'll count on you to teach me the ropes around here."

Conor heard a sudden intake of breath to his right and he turned to the woman who sat by the fire, holding his daughter on her lap. "And this is Charlotte Flaherty, my stepmom and"—he leaned down to ruffle Ali's hair—"my daughter, Alannah—Ali."

Sam offered her hand to Charlotte with a warm hello and then stooped down to Ali's level. "Hello, Ali. It's very nice to meet you."

Ali turned her head into Charlotte's shoulder, which

didn't surprise Conor in the least. She was always shy around new people; although, he'd worried his child might recognize Sam. It didn't seem as if she did and he heaved a little inward sigh of relief. They'd have had to come up with some new story on the spot if she'd realized Sam was the stranded driver from Sunday night.

"I met Sam when I was up at Sean's in June and we've been"—Conor paused for effect, giving Sam a meaningful glance—"staying in touch ever since." He stuck as close to the truth as he could—he did go up to Sean's in June and met Bren and Aidan there for their annual brothers' weekend. Last year, they'd met at Bren's in Washington, DC, and the year before in California at Aidan's Malibu beach cottage. Next year, he would host their event which would most likely be spent trimming vines and drinking wine. So it was possible he could have met Sam in June.

He didn't, but it was possible.

Once again, Megan was the first to recover. "It's so good you could join us, Sam. Would you like some mulled wine? It's a winter favorite all along the river."

Sam patted Conor's arm before following Meg to the impromptu buffet he'd set up earlier. He hoped the spread would impress Sam's foodie instincts. Potato-leek soup simmered in the slow cooker, its scent doing battle with the cinnamon spice of the heated wine that graced the opposite end of the table. In between, he'd placed a basket of bread and a couple sticks of butter, containers of chopped green onion, crumbled bacon, shredded cheese, and sour cream to dress up the soup, along with a stack of pottery bowls with plates, spoons, and knives, and a pile of napkins. Her box of cupcakes would fit perfectly in the only empty space left.

"Hey, Ali, look what Sam brought." He knelt down and pulled off the lid of the large bakery box, revealing a couple dozen of Paula Meadows's delicious cupcakes.

When Ali slipped off Charlotte's lap and ran to his side, the older woman's lips drew into a tight line. He wondered if she disapproved of this entire scene—a party on a school night even though it was only preschool, sugary treats before bedtime, and most of all, a stranger in their midst. With a mental shake of his head, he dismissed the thought—Char wasn't like that. At least she never had been, not in twelve years she and Da had been married.

Ali happily oohed and aahed over the treats as Sam stepped over, mug in hand to crouch down beside him.

"You can have any one you want, but I picked one just for you, Ali." She tilted her head and the scent of citrus and something else, something familiar and delicious and yet indefinable, floated toward him.

What is it? Her head was so close; he only had to lean ever so slightly to catch the fragrance again. Not roses, which was what Emmy had always worn. A bottle of Aerin Evening Rose still perched in the medicine chest in his bathroom, and the scent sometimes wafted out when he opened the closet door, even though all of Emmy's clothes were gone now.

"Can you guess which one it is?" Sam's voice was tinged with such delight that Conor's heart beat faster in his chest. She was either a remarkable actress or truly pleased to be interacting with his daughter. He leaned toward—hoped for—the latter.

Ali didn't hesitate a second. "The pink snowman!"

Sam chuckled. "That's right. Only after you eat supper, though." She rose and gently placed one hand on Ali's head and announced, "Let it be known to all and sundry that the pink snowman cupcake belongs to Miss Ali. Otherwise, I hope you all enjoy." Then she extended her hand to Ali. "Did I see a cat in the corner over there? What's his name?"

Ali held up two chubby fingers. "We have two kitties." She grabbed Sam's hand, pulling her toward the racks of wine along the wall. "This is Zin. He likes to be petted. See? He always turns over like that. Do you want to rub his tummy?"

Conor let the murmur of his guests' voices fall into background noise as he watched Sam gracefully settle on the floor without a moment of concern about getting her pants dusty, folding her long legs into what Ali called *crisscross applesauce*—the position he and his brothers had always referred to as *sitting Indian style*. Whatever it was called, Sam allowed Ali to dump a very tolerant Zin into her lap and demonstrate exactly where to pet his belly to make his motor run. The gray tabby proceeded to purr so loudly Conor could hear it from his position near the fireplace several feet away.

Normally not a social critter, Merlot, the long-haired calico suddenly appeared from her hideaway in the office, almost as if she sensed Zin might be getting some attention that as queen of the winery was rightfully hers. But then she disappeared again just as quickly.

"So, you want to fill me in here?" Tierney murmured, suddenly at his side.

She was never one for subtlety, but their friendship went back to grade school so he didn't really mind. As Emmy's best friend, she'd been right beside them throughout the evil cancer, particularly at the end. She'd slip in and take over the vigil for Conor when sorrow and exhaustion drove him from Emmy's bedside to catch a few hours of precious sleep on the living room sofa. And later, weeks after the funeral, Tierney had been the one his brothers had finally called to come drag him out of his room and into the sunshine. He wasn't going to be able to fool her.

Too aware of being within Charlotte's earshot, Conor merely shrugged and gave Tierney what he hoped was an enigmatic smile. Let her make of that what she would. He didn't want things to get too complicated, and he and Sam needed to be on the same page, so he wasn't going to expand on their story unless she was nearby.

"Come on, Conny, dish." Tierney, whose diminutive size never daunted her from getting what she wanted from a Flaherty, elbowed his ribs gently.

He tousled her dark curls affectionately—a gesture that would annoy and, with any luck, distract her. "There's no dish, Tee. She's a . . . a friend. And don't call me *Conny*."

Tierney slapped his hand away with an exasperated *har-rumph*. "A *friend*, huh?" She gazed at him, eyes narrowed, clearly trying to read more into his benign expression before shaking her head. "Okay, okay. Fortunately for you, we're in a crowd and I'm starving. We're coming back around to this, *mon ami*, and soon. Count on it." Her mock ire softened. "She *is* lovely, Con."

He merely nodded and slung an arm over his old friend's shoulder to lead her to the buffet. "I know."

SAM SAT ACROSS from Charlotte at one of the tall tables, but hadn't managed to get a word in edgewise because Ali had claimed a spot at the same table and had talked a mile a minute since they'd all taken their places. The older woman's affection for Conor's big-eyed daughter was obvious as she and Teresa Ashton, the fourth at their table, encouraged the little girl's chatter, bombarding her with questions that kept the child engaged while Sam ate quietly.

"Ali." Conor's deep voice interrupted a drawn-out story about a litter of kittens that had visited preschool that day. "More eating; less talking. Your soup's getting cold."

Sam had been too aware of him as he sat at the table

right behind her talking with the mayor and Frank and Tierney Ashton. Bits and pieces of their conversation had drifted in whenever Ali took a breath or a bite, and Sam had gathered they were discussing the annual Christmas Candlelight Walk that was apparently happening in a less than two weeks. She could imagine how beautiful the little river town would look with all the shops and homes lit up for the holiday and luminarias lining the sidewalks and streets. Maybe she could drive back down for it—*no! For heaven's sake, this town was bewitching her.*

"Am I too late?" A huge booming voice filled the winery on a rush of cold air from the front door. The man who was yanking a wool cap off a shock of white hair was so slight Sam couldn't believe the voice had come from him until he continued in the same gruff bass. "Sorry I'm late. Got delayed at the office." He tossed the hat and his wool coat on a nearby chair.

"Harry!" The group hailed the older gentleman in unison.

He appeared to be in his early seventies and wore a tan corduroy suit she was sure dated to the late sixties. His face was lined and leathery, and he leaned on a brass-topped walking stick as he made his way to the buffet. This guy was a character, no doubt about it.

"Hey, everyone!" Harry greeted them all with a wave of his stick before heading straight for the buffet as the others called out hellos and other words of welcome.

Conor was clearly happy to see the old man and shook his hand before pulling him into an affectionate hug, while Ali hopped out of her chair to throw herself into his arms.

"I'm so glad to see you, Harry!" She squeezed him tight. "Come and meet Sam. That's her real name, but she's a girl."

Sam stayed in her chair, aware that at five foot nine, she'd tower over him. She'd been that height since eighth grade and had learned early in life to carry herself with dignity, but not overwhelm shorter people immediately—especially men.

Ali tugged on his hand after he'd returned her boisterous embrace.

"Let Harry get some supper first, Alannah." Conor put a restraining hand on her head and glanced over at Sam.

Ali's rosebud mouth drew down into a frown and she released Harry, but not before informing him that he could have any cupcake he wanted except the pink snowman. "Sam brought that one 'specially for *me*." She thumped her chest with her thumb.

"I'll fill my plate and pick a different cupcake and then I'll come and meet this Sam guy." Harry tossed Sam a smile over Ali's head.

"She's not a *guy*, Harry!" Ali rolled her eyes in four-year-old exasperation. "I told you, she's a girl, see? That's her right there." She wagged her finger at Sam.

"Oh. Okay, I see she's a girl." Harry acknowledged Sam again, this time with a sly grin and a wink, before turning back to the buffet and a quiet conversation with Conor.

"Harry's our local attorney." Teresa's words brought Sam back around to face the table. "He's a fixture here. His father and grandfather before him served the town as lawyers and his dad was a circuit court judge for years before he passed."

"I see." Sam practically had to bite her tongue to keep from saying that she already knew exactly who Harry Evans was. His name was all over the documentation she'd received from Sean, and Donal Flaherty had mentioned him several times in his journals. Apparently, he and Harry were golfing buddies—that was, when Donal took the time to golf. From what she'd read, Conor's father had spent most of his time working in the vineyard or with his wife and sons.

"Harry and my husband were good friends." Charlotte's expression grew ever so slightly melancholy and she started to say something more, but closed her mouth with a snap. She was a lovely woman—blonde hair turning to silver, intelligent gray eyes behind a pair of fashionable eyeglasses, and a kind, open face. It was clear just from the short time Sam had spent with her that she enjoyed the winery and adored little Alannah. Sam's instincts about people were pretty well developed after several years as a family law attorney. There was nothing avaricious or conniving about Charlotte Flaherty, which made this lawsuit all the more a mystery.

Was it merely that she didn't want to leave Four Irish Brothers and her granddaughter? But she was welcome to stay; Donal had indicated that in his will, leaving her a home and an income that would last the rest of her life. Conor and Sean had both indicated they had no intention of tossing her out on her ear. Perhaps her children *were* behind the lawsuit as Conor had suggested.

"I'm sure both you and Harry must miss him terribly." Sam laid one hand gently on Charlotte's. "From what Conor has told me, he was a wonderful man."

"The best. I miss him every moment of every day." Tears shimmered in the older woman's eyes before she blinked and looked away.

Probably time to get off the subjects of deceased husbands and lawyers and judges.

Sam took a sip of delicious mulled wine before she said, "I saw they were putting up decorations in town when I stopped by the bakery."

"Oh, yes." Charlotte beamed, swiping at her cheeks with a napkin. "We do Christmas here with great enthusiasm." She cocked one perfectly plucked brow. "How long are you staying? The tree lighting on the square is this weekend. That's when Santa Claus arrives, and then the Christmas Candlelight Walk is December twelfth. The whole town is lit up, including luminarias along the sidewalks and the River Walk. Plus all the stores stay open late the whole month with sales and special events."

"On Christmas Eve, all the churches in town join together for one midnight candlelight service at St. Agnes's. It's beautiful," Teresa added, her blue eyes shining.

"Is that the big stone church on the square?" Sam kept an eye on Harry and Conor who were still chatting by the buffet, an anxious Ali hovering close by. She suspected Conor was filling the old attorney in on exactly who she was and why she was here.

She wasn't the only one watching the two men. Charlotte's eyes never left the pair as she responded politely to Sam's questions about the holiday celebration in River's Edge. Abruptly, she slipped off her chair. "I'm going to go grab a cupcake." She gave Sam a distracted smile. "I hope you brought plenty of chocolate ones."

She was gone before Sam could answer and Teresa just rolled her eyes and shook her head. "That poor woman's a mess."

"Really?" Turning to face Teresa put the buffet table in Sam's direct line of sight. Conor and Harry still stood there, Conor leaning down slightly to listen to whatever Harry was saying as the older man dressed his bowl of potato soup with green onion, shredded cheese, and the last of the crumbled bacon. "I imagine she's still grieving Conor's father."

"Oh, thanks to her kids, she hasn't had time to grieve." Teresa scraped her spoon in her bowl to get the last bite of thick, creamy soup.

It *was* delicious and the fact that Conor made it grew his appeal even more, if that was possible. Smart, handsome, successful, sexy, *and* he could cook. He was quickly turning into her ideal man.

Sam frowned suddenly as Teresa's word sunk in. "Her kids?"

Teresa's lips tightened. "Charlotte's been my best friend for almost twelve years. She's the sweetest, most sensible woman I know . . . except when it comes to her kids. I swear if one of those two parasites told her they needed her liver, she'd do the surgery herself with a paring knife and deliver it in a gift bag before she dropped over dead. They just—" She stopped, crumpled her napkin, and released an exasperated breath. "Sorry. I need to shut my big mouth." She forced an over-bright smile. "So how did you and Conor meet?"

Frustrated that the woman's better nature had suddenly taken over, Sam resigned herself to small talk. "Through his brother Sean. This is a charming little town. So they light up the path along the river, too?"

Eyes sparkling, Teresa set a hand on her arm for a moment. "Honey, they string white twinkle lights on anything that's standing still. My advice to you is to keep moving if you're downtown." She hopped down off her stool. "There's a chocolate cupcake calling my name. Can I bring you one?"

Just then, Conor appeared at Sam's side. "You seem like a key lime kind of woman to me, Ms. Hayes. Sweet and delicious, yet very . . . um . . . zesty." He presented her with a plate that held two tempting cupcakes.

How did he know?

"Me? I'm crazy about Paula's praline pecan." He plopped down in the seat Charlotte had vacated as Harry and Ali, chattering a mile a minute, settled in across the table. He held her eyes with a gaze so intimate, it nearly knocked Sam sideways. "It's those little differences that keep a relationship interesting, now, isn't it?"

Chapter Seven

"THERE." SAM PLACED one more candy cane, then stood back, brushed her hands together, and smiled up at the tall Douglas fir shimmering with white lights. They'd added red balls, silver bells, and candy canes to the wine-cork garland and strings of red and silver beads on the winery's Christmas tree. The effect was simple yet festive and just suited the rustic ambiance of Four Irish Brothers Winery. "You are perfectly . . . perfect," she whispered, gazing up at the lighted star glowing on top of the twelve-foot tree. She inhaled the fresh scent of pine and opened her arms as if to embrace the scene before her.

The guests were all gone now. However, everyone had pitched in with enthusiasm after supper. Pine garland was strung across the heavy beam that served as a mantel for the stone fireplace. Charlotte had tucked red-and-white gingham bows into the branches, adding to the country look. Nate and Frank Ashton got busy wrapping garland around the posts that held up the high roof, while Tierney and Teresa and Megan had decorated the tasting bar with swooping swags of holly and spruce. Even little Ali made sure every single votive cup centerpiece on each table glowed with an electric candle.

Sam, Conor, and Ali had mainly focused on the tree though, laughing together comfortably as they sorted through the boxes of decorations, unwinding the tangle of wine-cork garland and strings of silver sleigh bells. Sam delighted in Ali's chatter about holiday traditions in River's Edge as they hung ornaments and enjoyed a preview of the Christmas songs that the little girl's preschool class would sing on the square that weekend. She sensed Conor's warm gaze on her as she and Ali giggled and talked. Once when she looked up from placing a sprig of holly in Ali's ponytail, she caught him smiling an enigmatic smile that made her heart stutter.

Ali had stuck close to Conor and Sam right up to the moment Charlotte approached with a cautious smile. "I think it's past some little girl's bedtime, Daddy." She held out her hand to Ali. "I'll take her up in my cart and tuck her in if you like. That way you can stay here with your . . . guest." The older woman aimed a pointed glance in Sam's direction.

Ali's raced to Sam's side. "But tonight's special, Grammy Char, so I get to stay up later." She tossed a pleading look in Conor's direction, and Sam couldn't help noticing how beautiful the child's eyes were—deep brown shot with gold, like amber. Were her mother's eyes that chocolate and honey color?

Conor checked the big clock above the fireplace. "Sorry, kiddo. We're already half an hour past your bedtime. You better say your good nights and head up to the house with Grammy."

Ali pouted and clung to Sam. "Pleeease, Da, Sam and I still have to finish hanging up the stockings and I want to find Merlot and show Sam her freckles." Tears glistened in her eyes, threatening to spill over onto her rosy cheeks.

Sam wasn't sure whether she should interfere, but after a few more minutes of tearful negotiation on Ali's part and kind yet firm words from Conor, she unwound the little girl's arms from around her waist. Crouching down to look into her face, she said earnestly, "Hey, listen, Ali. Why don't you go with Grammy Char now and I promise I'll come back tomorrow after you get home from school and you can show me Merlot's freckles then. I've never seen a cat with freckles before. Your dad and I will finish hanging up the stockings tonight, so the winery will be all done and we can spend our time with Zin and Merlot. Would that be okay?"

With a sniff and a side eye to Charlotte, who had waited silently in the background throughout the entire exchange, Ali finally relented, but not before she hurled herself into Sam's arms. "I like you," she whispered in Sam's ear as she hugged her close. "Want to be best friends?"

Sam's heart swelled as, "I like you, too, sweetie," came out a little choky.

Her experience with kids was pretty much limited to the

children of the clients she represented in custody cases, and those were rarely happy situations. None of her friends had children yet and being an only child, she didn't have nieces or nephews. She was surprised how easily she'd fallen into a rhythm with Ali in just a couple of hours. The girl had charmed her almost as much as her dad did, which was saying a lot.

The evening had been a huge success as far as decorating the tasting room was concerned, although for Sam, not so much in getting to know Charlotte. Conor's stepmother had spent most of her time sequestered with Teresa in the small kitchen behind the office, cleaning up the dishes from supper. It almost seemed as if Charlotte was avoiding her. That was ridiculous, of course . . . unless she resented the idea of her stepson dating or Sam's immediate rapport with Ali. Either way it was disconcerting.

"Are you talking to my Christmas tree?" Conor's deep voice interrupted her musing.

She laughed over her shoulder. "What if I am?"

Ordinarily, the teasing lilt in her voice would've felt foreign to her ear, but here, in this place with this man, it was comfortable and relaxed. In Sam's limited experience, men were never easy, and relationships, especially the getting-to-know-you parts, were arduous, which was why she'd avoided serious dating since David had broken up with her. Yet with Conor, she'd been so drawn to him that the usual awkwardness had never appeared.

"I guess I'll only worry if that thing talks back to you, eh?" He grinned and a sweet, heady flush that had nothing to do with the heat from the fireplace coursed down her body.

He sauntered closer, a bottle of wine and two stemmed glasses in one hand. "Nightcap?"

"Sure." She settled onto a stool at the nearest table. "Just one glass, though. I have to drive back to town and, as you well know, the road to the Serendipity is curvy and goes downhill all the way to Main Street."

Expertly, he uncorked the bottle, poured a half-inch of rich red liquid into a glass, and set it in front of her. "Swirl, sniff, and sip."

"Is this a test?" She picked up the wide-bowl glass by the stem and watched the wine coat the inside as she swirled. "I do get more than this, right?" She looked up at him from under her lashes, dumbfounded once again at how Conor Flaherty brought out the flirty girl in her. That part of Sam had been buried under long days as a new associate at the law firm and trying to be the perfect daughter and the perfect attorney. In the last year, she'd kept it tucked safely away as she focused totally on her work. How had it surfaced so quickly?

"Hold tight. This is only to taste it." He winked as he poured an equally small amount into his own glass. "Just tell me what you smell. Put your nose in the glass."

"Okay." Sam put her nose down and inhaled deeply. "I

don't know . . . cherries? Raspberries?" When he gave her an approving nod, she sniffed again. "Vanilla and . . . maybe some kind of spice? Is there a hint of tobacco?"

He grinned. "Probably. It's our chambourcin from several years ago. We've only got a few cases left. This wine can be fruity and intense and usually ends with a little peppery spice, so you've totally got it. They call this grape the Pennsylvania zinfandel, but it can sometimes be acidic, so we age it in American oak. That's where the aromas of earth and tobacco and vanilla come from." He touched his glass to hers in salute. "Okay, now taste. Don't gulp it down; hold it in your mouth for a second before you swallow."

"Are you seriously teaching me how to drink wine?" Sam couldn't resist teasing him. "I'm from Chicago. My dad took me all over Northern California once just for wine tasting. I know what a good red wine should taste like, Mr. Flaherty."

"Oh, I get it. You're a big-city girl. You already know all this stuff, right?" He brushed his hair off his forehead and caught his lower lip between his teeth in a move so startlingly sensual, it nearly took Sam's breath away. "You've never had *my* best red wine. Just taste it."

Obediently, she tipped her glass, savoring the complex flavors of one of the finest dry reds she'd ever tasted. For one brief moment, she wished her dad was there. He'd always preferred California reds, but this one . . . Conor Flaherty had made a perfect wine. "My gosh! At first . . . subtle . . . like cloves and berries and jam. The end is"—she sipped again, holding the wine against her tongue before swallowing—"the end is huge. Pepper and . . . and raisins?" She met his gaze over the rim of her glass. "Conor, this is amazing."

"It is, isn't it?" Delight shone in his blue eyes and he poured them both a full measure of wine.

She sipped again. "We need chocolate."

AND THAT ONE comment clinched it. Conor desperately wanted, no *needed*, to get to know this woman better. Her expressive eyes had taken him in from the moment he'd met them over her shredded tire. The fiercely independent spirit that clearly did battle with her common sense when she accepted his help had piqued his curiosity—the first time a woman had done that in ages. She'd stayed with him even after they'd gone their separate ways, unaware they'd be meeting again in just a few hours. The fact that they'd hit it off during their meeting that morning had intrigued him, but her easy and immediate connection with Ali while they decorated the tree surprised the hell out of him. And although he'd rather cut his own tongue out than tell her, she *was* overdressed for the party. Unquestionably he was going to find out if she even owned a pair of jeans, but seeing that she truly was an unabashed foodie and oenophile enchanted him beyond words.

"You really do have a terrific palate." He held up one

finger. "Don't move."

He ran over to the office to grab the two small squares of Ghirardelli dark chocolate that were stacked on his desk. He couldn't remember offhand where they'd come from. He'd been saving them for the next time he opened a bottle of the 2010 chambourcin. And, yes, opening that particular wine had been a test—one she'd just passed with flying colors.

"Okay, now take a bite of chocolate, let it melt on your tongue, and sip the wine over it." He unwrapped one of the squares and held it up. He expected her to take it in her fingers; instead, she just leaned down and bit off a piece. Her mouth touched his thumb and finger for an instant, and a tingle zinged right through him.

He looked down at her, hoping she hadn't felt him shiver, but her eyes were closed as she savored the mix of chocolate and rich red wine. He ate the other half of the square of dark chocolate, took a drink of wine, and shook himself mentally as the flavors blended on his tongue.

Get a grip! You've known this woman for all of a day and she's not here for your pleasure. She's here to save your damn business.

Women flirted with him all the time. It was inevitable in a small town where single men were in short supply. Although he didn't think of himself as a "catch," a thirty-three-year-old widower was still something of a novelty in River's Edge.

For the last two years, Conor had learned to sidestep,

smile, and be polite while he focused on Ali and the winery. And if the temptation to fix the physical ache welled up in him now and again, that desire was quashed at the idea of kissing a woman who wasn't Emmy. Accepting a quick night of what Da would've called *canoodling* would have been a very temporary and most certainly disastrous solution to an age-old problem. Conor frequently wished Da were still around to dispense some Irish wisdom about widowers and urges and fixing physical needs.

This woman, though? Ah, this woman was something entirely different, and if he hadn't already been a goner, the look on her face as she enjoyed his wine would've done it.

She opened her eyes and he was lost in their depths. "Mmmm. This is wonderful! What is it about dark chocolate and wine? The combination is . . . I don't know how to describe it."

Seductive. He wasn't about to offer the word that came immediately to his mind. Instead, he had to look away from her. He was sure his expression would've sent her running terrified out of the winery . . . and out of his life. He gazed at the fire for a moment.

Yeah, seductive *is definitely the word.*

She reached for the other square of chocolate and unwrapped it. As she offered the piece to him, it began to slide from her fingers. It slipped from her grip, but his hand was already by hers, and he snatched it before it fell to the tabletop. Resisting the urge to feel her lips on his fingers again, he simply broke the candy into two pieces and handed her half. She chuckled and was about to say something when he stopped her.

"Hold still." He extended a hand to her cheek. As he reached toward her, her eyes widened and she pulled away a little, and then stopped. "Chocolate," he said, as his fingertip touched her cheek just next to her mouth to wipe the small streak of chocolate from her skin. For the first time since they'd met, there was an awkward silence between them as he realized how desperately he wanted to kiss her.

Before he could wrap his head around that thought, she set her glass down and sighed. "I'd better get back down to town. I have a meeting with Harry tomorrow and I want to go over some notes."

"Do you need me to be there?"

"No, this is just background stuff. Sean suggested I meet with Donal's lawyer, even though Harry recused himself from acting as attorney on this case."

"Yeah, he and his wife, Dee, played euchre with Da and Char once a week for years before Dee passed last year. The four of them were close friends." He shoved the cork down in the bottle and handed it to her. "Here, take this with you and enjoy it. My gift for helping out tonight." He pushed harder, making sure the cork was secure before pulling a corkscrew out of his jeans pocket and offering it to her. "And here. I'm assuming you aren't packing a wine opener. Most people don't."

Sam's grin lit up her face. "I'm not most people." She rose, crossed the room to her purse, reached into a side pocket, and held up a hot pink corkscrew—one he was sure had to have come from some breast cancer awareness event.

Once again, he was struck by how beautiful she was, her rich auburn hair picking up light from the candles on the tables, her amazing eyes sparkling with humor and warmth, and the graceful way she carried her slim frame. He laughed with her as he helped her on with her coat at the door of the winery, and found himself unsettled in a most remarkable way at the temptation to stroke her hair when he straightened her collar.

She glanced up at him, then smiled shyly as her gaze was snagged by something above his head.

The mistletoe!

Nate must have hung it up after he and his dad had wrapped pine swags around the posts earlier. Conor hadn't even noticed it until now. A pang went through him. The first kiss under the winery mistletoe had always belonged to him and Emmy. Then he blinked. The pang vanished almost as quickly as it had appeared when Sam chuckled softly.

She tilted her head and when she spoke, they were so close, her breath danced over his lips, sending a shiver down his spine. "Thanks for tonight, Conor."

He knew without a doubt he was going to kiss her; hell, he was *dying* to kiss her. He hitched his chin toward the mistletoe, asking permission with the quirk of one brow.

When she responded with the briefest of nods, he touched his mouth to hers. The kiss was slow. Sweet. Tender.

A new and different sensation surged through him as their lips met again and clung. Suddenly something was repaired where the ragged tear in his heart had been.

Chapter Eight

SAM ROSE UP on one elbow and turned her pillow over to the cool side for the fifth time since she'd crawled into bed—she glanced at the clock on the nightstand—over three hours ago! *Well, this is stupid.* Clearly, she wasn't going to sleep anytime soon. Throwing off the covers, she grabbed her sweater from the chair where she'd dropped it earlier and shrugged it on over her pajamas. She padded barefoot to the window and opened the plantation blinds to stare out at the wide Ohio River.

The waning moon still lit a pale path across the water, and stars, too numerous to count, filled the clear sky. It was a chilly night, but she lifted the window anyway and sat down on the deep, cushioned seat. There was a clarity to this moment; the air was clean and vibrant, and the smell of the pines and the *whooshing* sound of the river made her senses hum. Struck again at how alive she felt here, she wondered if the dull duties of a responsible life had blanketed her senses and her soul.

She wasn't foolish enough to believe it was merely the warm welcome she'd received from nearly everyone she'd

met or the quaint hominess of River's Edge that had capti-
vated her. It was also how quickly she'd been drawn to
Conor Flaherty. Not just an attraction, although dear Lord,
that was evident enough, but also an immediate . . . She
ransacked her vocabulary for the right word.

Was it *kinship*? In the few hours they'd spent together, he
seemed like someone who had no expectations, who simply
seemed happy to get to know her—plain Sam Hayes—not
the high-powered Chicago attorney. It *was* that part of her
life that brought them together, although they'd actually
connected before they'd ever discussed the lawsuit—even
before they'd known who each other was.

He'd touched something inside her when he'd stopped in
the pouring rain to help her. When he'd turned his car
around so his daughter would be able to keep him in her
sights, she'd seen her own dear father in his concern. Then
her heart had skipped a beat when he'd been so excited about
his wine that he'd insisted she taste it—before he'd discovered who she was. As they'd talked, she'd begun to realize
they were in the same place in life—wary, wondering, trying
to figure out what came next.

The ruse they'd concocted for the tree-trimming party
hadn't felt like playacting—a fact that left Sam confused and
exhilarated and nervous. And then there was the kiss. She
could still feel the imprint of his lips on hers. In the self-
conscious moment after he'd kissed her a second time, his
blue eyes had darkened slightly and if she hadn't pulled away

from him, his lips would have been on hers again . . . *and how delicious would that have been?* However, she'd merely touched his cheek, whispered *good night*, and left, certain in the knowledge he could have had her right then and there if he'd kissed her again. Her heart hurt, knowing it would have been a huge mistake.

Rising from the window seat, she wandered to the dresser and uncorked the bottle of wine he'd given her. The only glass she had was in the bathroom, rimmed with toothpaste, and she didn't feel like rinsing it out, so she shrugged, tipped the bottle up, and took a swig. She held the wine in her mouth for a moment, relishing the mellow, yet rich flavor before she swallowed and carried the bottle to the window. She'd never had chambourcin before—man, it *was* tasty.

Both her father and Conor would be appalled to see her drinking directly out of the bottle, but she didn't care. The wine relaxed her, so she took another drink. The fact was she hadn't been prepared for Conor Flaherty to be so damn attractive or to affect her like he had. She pressed her hand against her belly, trying to ease the ache at the thought of him only a few miles away. Tonight at the party and especially under the mistletoe, it almost seemed like he could have been having some of the same feelings. The thought gave her a sudden surge of pleasure, then she shook her head at her own silliness. He was only caught up in the moment— just as she had been. She took another long drag of wine and let the liquid warm her right down to her toes before she leaned her forehead against the cool, rippled glass of the old window.

You're here as his attorney, Sam. Do your job and get back to real life. Time to woman up and be the attorney you know you can be.

Why was she allowing this town, this man to draw her in? Was it the anxiety left over from Charlie Brigg's brutal attack on his family or was it something more? Something she'd been longing for, but had denied in her quest for her mother's approval. Sam raked her fingers through her hair and heaved a frustrated sigh.

The hearing was in ten days. All she had to do was stay focused and build the argument for the defense and she could do that in Chicago. This research trip really only had to be a few days. No need to get sidetracked. This chemistry that kept flaring up between them didn't matter. Conor was firmly planted here in this town, in his vineyard, and she was very definitely ensconced in her life and career in Chicago—something she had no intention of changing. Especially over a mild flirtation with the local winemaker.

Mild flirtation? Her conscience nudged.

"Yes!" she said aloud, taking another long drink before shoving the cork back into the bottle with a little more force than necessary. The urge to call Aunt Bette and process all of this with someone who knew her almost better than she knew herself was quelled when she glanced at the clock. Although Bette would pick up and stay on the phone with

Sam as long as she needed to talk, it was well past midnight. Besides, there was nothing to process. A couple of innocent kisses under the mistletoe didn't mean anyone was turning their life upside down.

She closed the window, lowered the blind, and set the bottle of Conor Flaherty's best wine back on the dresser. Shivering, she slipped back into the big warm bed and pulled the covers up to her chin.

CONOR PACED THE length of the living room in the log home that he and Emmy had built on the hill across the vineyard from the winery. The log house they'd intended to fill with children. The dimming moonlight shone on the rows of vines that separated his two lives—being a dad and being a winemaker. Those two things were his focus and yet, in less than two days, he'd become distracted. So distracted that he was, at this moment, picturing an auburn-haired, brown-eyed temptress curled up in one of Rose's king-sized beds. What did she wear to bed? Pajamas? A lacy nightgown? Or did she sleep in only a T-shirt and panties as Emmy had done for years?

His experience with women's nightwear was pretty limited, but he had no problem imagining tall, luscious Sam Hayes in a satin nightgown that revealed more than it covered. He closed his eyes and there she was, hair tousled, her eyes sleepy-sexy as she beckoned him with a lift of her chin. His entire body tightened at that picture and he groaned softly.

He ached with wanting . . . with needing to be touched. The sensation astounded him. His senses had been dormant for so long, he'd believed this was how his life without Emmy was going be. He'd grown accustomed to the emptiness that had replaced those particular yearnings. Now, in mere hours, they'd suddenly been roused. Although this wasn't simply a need to relieve some long-suppressed physical release. This was his soul awakening.

Turning away from the window, he caught sight of the picture of Emmy that sat on the lamp table by the leather sofa. Gazing at the photo, he picked it up and dropped to the couch with it in his hand. Blonde and tiny, she always made him think of an angel—the irony of which wasn't lost on him now.

"Is it you? Are you doing this to me, Emma Grace?" he whispered. "I know I promised you I'd get married again, find Ali a new mother, but I had my fingers crossed behind my back the whole time."

He stroked the face of the photo, and waited for the lump that usually formed in his throat to appear. It didn't.

Instead, he smiled. "I think you knew that, didn't you? Are you up there pushing me?"

"Da?" A small voice from the bottom of the stairs startled him out of his reverie.

He held out his arms and Ali ran into them. "What are you doing up, poppet?" Conor had taken to using the nickname his father had given Ali the day she was born. Donal's brogue seemed to come out in him when he said it and he liked that. "It's late."

"I listened to my body and got up to pee. Then I looked over the rail and saw you down here." Ali snuggled against Conor's flannel shirt. "Where are your jammies, Da?"

"I haven't gotten ready for bed yet." He settled her onto his lap, loving the scent of her dark hair that Charlotte had braided for bed. "Good for you, sweets. I'm glad you listened to your body."

"Were you talking to Mommy in heaven?" Ali touched his stubbled cheek.

"I was." Conor caught her tiny fingers in his and pressed a kiss into her palm.

"Do you miss her a lot?"

"I do. I miss her every day."

"Like I miss *Daideó*?" Ali's pronunciation of the Irish word for grandfather came out *Daddy-O*, which charmed the socks off the entire family.

They'd all taken to calling Donal *Daddy-O* after the first time she'd said it. Aidan had even made a chuckle ripple across the congregation when he shared the *Daddy-O* story at Donal's memorial service, and with tears and laughter, the four brothers had toasted their *Daddy-O* with chambourcin in the wine cellar that night.

"I imagine it's a lot like that," Conor said. "I miss him, too."

Ali lay quietly in his arms for a few minutes and he thought she'd fallen back asleep when suddenly she piped up. "Da, I think we need a new mommy."

Conor blinked.

Where's this coming from?

"Why do you think we need a new mommy?" He lifted her chin gently to stare into her face. God, she was looking more like Emmy every day in spite of the difference in their hair color.

"Kyle has a new mommy, so now he has two." Ali twisted her face from Conor's fingers. "And two daddies."

"Oh, I see." Conor remembered Sherri and Phil Sargent, Kyle's parents divorced not long after Emmy had died. He hadn't really kept up with them, although he vaguely remembered Phil bringing a very young woman into the winery one day last summer. Apparently, Sherri had remarried, too.

"I think Sam would be a good mommy." Ali sat up to stare into his face in the shadows of the one lamp he had lit.

"Do you?" He bit his lip to keep from smiling.

"Yup." Ali nodded vigorously. "She's nice and she's so pretty."

"Honey, Sam and I only just met. You don't marry someone you just met. You need to get to know them, spend time with them."

"How long did you know Mommy before you married her?"

"Mommy and I met in the eighth grade."

"And then you got married?" Ali's eyes sparkled with curiosity.

Conor suspected she was buying time so she didn't have to go back to bed, but he decided to see where it went. "No, we didn't get married until after we both went to college, so that was like eight years after we met."

"Mommy went to college?" Ali rested her arm on his chest, her chin in her palm. "And you did too?"

He nodded. "Yup. Mommy learned to be a teacher and I learned to be a winemaker, remember? We talked about this before."

"I know, but sometimes I forget." Ali gave him the little imp smile that did him in every time. "Why did you go to college to learn to be a winemaker when *Daideó* could teach you?"

"Well, there's a lot of science to making wine, and *Daideó* wanted me to go to Purdue and learn the science part so we could make our wine even better."

"I don't like wine very much," Ali confessed, then gasped and clapped her hand over her mouth.

Conor tried to look stern. "How do you know that?" He was pretty sure he already knew the answer.

"Uncle Aidan let me have a little drink of his at Thanksgiving. I heard him tell Uncle Sean that kids like me drink wine in some other places. Maybe, um, Fr-France?" She clasped her hands together. "Don't be mad at him. Uncle Bren already yelled at him."

He wasn't one bit surprised it was Aidan who'd given his daughter wine. His little brother was wrapped around the girl's finger, as were all the rest of them. "I won't be mad at him. But in this place, wine is for grownups, okay?"

"Okay. I didn't like it anyway." Ali yawned and settled back against his chest. "Da, did Mommy know me?"

"Of course she knew you, poppet." Conor bit his lip, knowing where this line of questioning was headed. Ali loved to hear the stories about the time she spent as a baby with her mother. He waited for Ali's next inevitable words.

"But . . . but I don't remember her." Ali rubbed her cheek on his shirt and curled her knees to her chest. "I want to, but I can't make a picture of her face in my head."

He drew the little girl closer and pressed his lips against the top of her head. "You were only two when she went to heaven, that's why I put the picture of her on your dresser."

They'd had this conversation several times lately. Not the part about needing a new mommy, that was new and different, but the retelling of the Ali-and-Emmy story. How Ali sat on Emmy's sickbed in the guest room, cuddling with her mommy while they read stories, played with little toys, and sang silly songs and lullabies. How when he'd come to take Ali up to bed, Emmy's tears had tugged at his heart so much, he finally set up a portable crib next to her hospital bed, so the two of them could share a room.

A lump formed in his throat as memories of those final days washed over him and he swallowed hard, waiting for the ache in his heart. It was different this time. Not the usual melancholy that preceded days of gloom; rather a sweet sadness filled him at the memory of his angel-wife crooning to their daughter until her chemo-raspy voice gave out. God, how he missed her, but the pain was finally easing, due perhaps in some small way to the arrival of Sam Hayes.

Ali shifted in his arms. "Can we ask Sam to go with us to the Christmas tree lighting in town?" she asked.

"Maybe." Conor tipped his head to stare at his child, amazed all over again at the love that welled up in him. "I'm not sure she'll still be here."

"She will be. It's in five days and for sure she'll want to stay for it." Another jaw-cracking yawn and Ali's eyelids drooped. "I think she likes us."

"We'll see." Conor didn't see the point in getting Ali's hopes up, or his own for that matter, since Sam had merely whispered good night and left after he'd kissed her under the mistletoe. As the grandfather clock in the corner struck midnight, he gathered his sleeping daughter in his arms, rose, and headed up the stairs.

Chapter Nine

"COULDA KNOCKED ME over with a feather when Conor showed me the letter from that fancy-pants Louisville lawyer. Never would've believed it of Charlotte." Harry Evans stared into a pottery mug for a second or two, then shrugged and filled it with steaming dark liquid from the ancient drip coffeemaker on the credenza behind his desk. "Cream? Sugar?" He held up the mug.

"Um, a little cream, please." Wondering when the mug had last been washed, Sam managed not to cringe as she accepted the cup, then mentally rolled her eyes at how much she sometimes was exactly like her mother. Except Mother would accept the coffee, set it aside, and never drink it, while Sam was dying for another shot of caffeine this morning. Surely the hot coffee would kill any stray germs.

He filled his own mug and plopped back into the big leather desk chair. His office might have been a movie set for an old-country-lawyer scene. The furniture was heavy dark mahogany with brass fittings. A framed diploma above the coffeemaker showed Harry had graduated from Harvard School of Law in 1968, and a quick mental calculation on

Sam's part put him at about seventy-four if he'd gone straight through from college. She wondered idly if he had children. There was a photo of him and a lovely woman on the credenza behind his desk, but no other pictures of children or grandchildren.

Bookcases lined two walls of the office and overflowed with volumes on every possible aspect of the law as well as an entire shelf devoted to fly-fishing, one filled with tattered travel guides, and an array of fiction that ranged from John Grisham's thrillers to Sue Grafton's alphabet mystery series. Anyone who was a fan of Kinsey Millhone was okay in Sam's eyes. She and Aunt Bette had devoured the series and were both heartbroken when Grafton died before she could write *Z is for . . .*

She took a sip of the fragrant brew. It was amazingly good. "This coffee is delicious."

"It's Kona—I order the beans special from a coffee plantation that I discovered in Hawaii a few years ago. Can't buy it anywhere else." He closed his eyes as he took a drink. "And don't be fooled by Kona blends in coffee shops and the grocery. They only have to contain about ten percent Kona to be called *Kona blend*. This is one hundred percent Kona." He grinned and Sam thought what a hottie he must have been back in the day. He was still a darn handsome man, although she preferred her men with more meat on their bones and taller . . . and younger. More like Conor Flaherty, actually.

Focus, Sam. Lawsuit.

"I'm not entirely sure what to ask you." She reached for a cork coaster with a faded picture of a roller coaster on it that was on the desk and set her coffee down. "I mean, you're Donal's attorney. You took care of all his business; however, you've recused yourself from *this* suit."

"I had to." Harry leaned back in his chair. "I'm too close to Charlotte. Ethically, I can't talk to you as an attorney today. I'm talking to you as Charlotte and Donal's friend."

Sam nodded and pulled out the small leather-bound notebook she kept in her purse. "Do you mind if I take some notes while we talk?"

"No, just remember, this conversation is off the record. If you want me to testify or be a character witness, subpoena me." A sip or two of coffee later, he folded his hands on his desk and took a deep breath. "Here's the thing. In my own personal opinion, Charlotte doesn't want to do this."

"But she *is* doing it." Sam had the paperwork in her briefcase to prove it, so Harry's opinion, although interesting, didn't change anything.

"I know." Harry raised one bushy white brow and tugged at the ends of his moustache.

She waited for a moment, hoping he'd add more without her having to pull it out of him with leading questions. He didn't.

Instead he chuckled. "Conor tells me you're from Sean's high-powered practice in Chicago. Divorce and family law.

You in the business of taking rich cheating husbands to the cleaners, Ms. Hayes?" His smirk told her he'd probably researched her role at the law firm of Stark, Randolph, Smith, and Flaherty. No doubt he'd googled her and discovered the fact that, thanks to the Chicago press, she was known as *The Dragon Lady* when it came to divorce cases.

"Why don't you tell me why you believe Charlotte doesn't really want to contest Donal's will." She sidestepped Harry's curiosity.

She wasn't going to get drawn into a discussion about her career. She was a damn fine divorce attorney; she simply needed a break from all the ugliness of unhappy couples. Sean sent her down here to take care of another kind of custody fight, to save his family's winery, and by God, she intended to do just that. First though, she needed to figure out Charlotte Flaherty.

Harry sat up straight and set his palms on his desk. "Charlotte loves Donal's boys like they are her own kids. When Donal remarried, the whole town thought the boys would never accept her. They all worshipped Maggie. He waited to start dating until Aidan was eighteen and graduated from high school, although I don't think that was deliberate. He was just very focused on raising the boys and keeping the winery growing. Charlotte happened into the winery when he was more or less taking a breath."

"Did you think she was a gold digger? I mean, when you first met her?"

He let out a bark of laughter. "No way. Charlotte Flaherty is the furthest thing from a gold digger I've ever known. You must've discovered from your research that she's perfectly comfortable with the money her husband left her when he passed. If you didn't, you haven't done your homework."

Sam let out a quick gust of air. "I do know what her finances are like. She doesn't *need* money, but this lawsuit certainly indicates that she *wants* it. So what do *you* think she's after?"

"Frankly, I think her kids, two of the most ungrateful, entitled brats you'll ever meet, have convinced her that Conor and his brothers intend to toss her out on her ear." Harry rose, refilled both their cups, and passed the carton of half-and-half to Sam.

"Donal's will clearly states she's welcome to stay in the homestead for the remainder of her life or for as long as she cares to. Why would she believe her kids?" Sam took a sip of coffee, inhaling the incredible scent as she drank.

"Robert and Sabrina are twins and as far as I can tell, neither of them has done an honest day's work in their lives. They're almost thirty years old and although they both had offices in their father's bank, they rarely showed up. They spend most of their time on beaches and at ski resorts. From what I understand, Char's husband spoiled them rotten and let them run over poor Char like steamrollers. According to Donal, marrying him was the first thing she ever did that went against her kids' wishes."

Sam scribbled in her notebook as questions brewed in her mind, but she simply nodded, encouraging Harry to continue.

"Both the twins were ousted by the bank board when it was bought up by a much larger bank not long after their dad died. The free ride ended."

"I know their father left them money. I saw his will." As Sam recalled, Charlotte's children each inherited a tidy sum from their dad. Even if they'd lost their jobs, they still should've been fine.

"Those two live way beyond their means—always have, I think." Harry shook his head. "My opinion is that they're either money seeking or making sure they never have to take care of their mother. That would put a crimp in their lifestyles for sure."

"Sean says he and his brothers fear that if they have to give Charlotte a piece of the winery, then when she passes, the kids will inherit that piece and be in control of a fifth of the business." It was a question wrapped up in a rather leading statement—the kind Sam had mastered after eight years as a divorce attorney to some of the wealthiest women in Chicago. She didn't know for sure if Harry was Charlotte's attorney; however, she assumed that if he'd done Donal's will, there was a good chance, he'd also done Charlotte's. He really couldn't reveal what was in Charlotte's will. That would be a breach of ethics.

The old attorney was too wily to get caught up in what

seemed like an innocent observation. He just shrugged one shoulder. "Or Robert and Sabrina could convince her to sell her portion to a larger concern. Donal had been approached several times by one of these new wine conglomerates that are buying up small boutique wineries. He didn't want his wine sitting on grocery store shelves, and I know Conor feels the same way. A few local restaurants serve Four Irish Brothers, but they don't retail outside of their own tasting rooms."

"What big company would want one-fifth of a local winery?"

"Maybe none, but it would be a foot in the door." Harry took a long drink of coffee. "And it would cause trouble for the boys."

"If she loves them so much, why would she want to do that?"

"I truly believe her kids have railroaded her once again." Harry pursed his lips and his bushy white moustache quivered. "She's a good woman, but those two play her like a fine violin. She just can't see them for who they truly are."

"What kind of relationship do the boys have with Robert and Sabrina?" Sam had posed the same question to both Sean and Conor and gotten pretty much the same response—an eye roll and a shrug. According to them, their contact with Charlotte's jet-setting kids had been limited to the occasional holiday dinner or running into one of them when they deigned to visit their mother. They'd turned up at

Donal's funeral however, suddenly turning into hovering and concerned children. Sam wanted an outsider's opinion of the step-family dynamics.

"Oh, Donal made an effort to try to blend the families when he and Char were first married and I'm certain the boys were open to it. They liked her immediately and were ready to embrace her kids." Harry shoved his chair back and picked up both their empty mugs. "But until Donal's death, Robert and Sabrina were rarely around. When they were, they're both such little snots, I don't think any of the boys regret not getting to know them better, although they all fell in love with Char. Anyway, except for Conor, the Flaherty boys are scattered across the country. They were definitely not going to become one big happy family with Rob and Sabrina."

In an instant, he switched gears. "You hungry? Let's go to Mac's and get some eggs."

"HARRY!" THE SMALL crowd in the diner greeted them as Harry held the door for her and the enticing odor of bacon and coffee wafted out. Sam had eaten one of Rose's amazing blueberry muffins earlier that morning and had already drunk enough coffee to float a barge, but her stomach growled anyway.

She had a sense of stepping back in time as she glanced

around the vast space filled with red vinyl booths and Formica tables. A vintage jukebox stood in one corner and a long counter with red stools separated the dining area from the kitchen. An attractive man with a bandana tied around his graying hair slipped out of the kitchen. "Harry! Where've you been, dude? Got your omelet all ready to pour, just waiting for your cheese choice."

Sam couldn't help noticing how nicely the guy filled out his jeans and white chef's jacket. Aunt Bette would call him a silver fox.

"I think gruyere this morning, Mac." Harry took Sam's jacket, hung it with his on the metal coatrack by the door, and patted the stool next to the one he slipped onto. "And another of your special omelets for my friend here."

"Oh, no . . ." Sam protested feebly, sounding as unconvinced as she felt. Just the scent of whatever Mac was cooking back there practically had her drooling. "I had a muffin at Rose's earlier and—" She snapped her mouth closed as Mac slapped a brightly colored menu down in front of her.

"Pick any three. More than three makes the omelet too busy and you can't appreciate the blend of flavors. Coffee?"

Harry jerked a thumb at Sam and grinned. "Switch her to water since she's already tasted Kona nirvana over at my place. Hate to ruin that with the swill you serve, but yeah, I'll take a cup."

Mac's toothy grin belied the middle finger he aimed at

Harry and, once again, Sam was struck by the camaraderie of this little river town. She scanned the list of ingredients that could be added to an omelet, trying to narrow it down to just three. "How about the roasted mushrooms, spinach, and gruyere?"

"You bet. Sweetheart, I'm going to Paris this bad boy up for you," Mac said with gusto. His energy nearly knocked Sam off her stool. "Add my special seasoning to it. You're gonna love it. And because it's Tuesday"—he turned to the remaining diners and raised his arms as though he was about to conduct a symphony—"what do we get with our eggs?"

In unison they all responded like school kids, "Baguette with truffle butter!"

He fist-pumped. "Exactly, my children. It's Truffle Butter Tuesday!" Mac leapt over the gate at the end of the counter. "You all make me so proud."

Harry grabbed Mac's sleeve as he passed. "Mac!"

The high-spirited chef skidded to a stop and raised one eyebrow. He had the greenest eyes Sam had ever seen with enough laugh crinkles around them to convince her this exuberance was his personality. She wanted to grab her phone, take a picture of this incredibly vibrant man, and send it to Aunt Bette, who would undoubtedly swoon.

"Meet Sam Hayes." Harry kept the introduction short, Sam assumed, because Mac was on the move again. "Friend of Sean and Conor's from Chicago."

Mac stopped, backed up, extended his hand, and shook

hers with vigor. "Hello, Sam Hayes. Welcome to my humble diner."

Sam returned his infectious grin. "From what I've heard, there's nothing humble about it."

His attempt at a modest smile failed miserably. "Well, we do try to keep the menu interesting."

"You have truffle butter for breakfast."

"And you're gonna love it!" Mac scooted back into the kitchen, singing the old Joe Walsh tune "Life's Been Good" in a decent, lusty baritone.

"I see you met Dad." Megan Mackenzie tapped Sam on the shoulder and plopped down on the stool on her other side. "What's he making you? Never mind, it's before noon, you're getting an omelet."

"I am." Sam nodded and shook her head. "This place is amazing. It's like going back to the fifties, except with gourmet fare. And your dad"—she inclined her head toward the kitchen where Mac was still singing as he whipped eggs—"I'm . . . I'm enchanted."

"Yeah. He has that effect." Megan slid off her stool, went around the end of the counter, washed her hands, and poured coffee into a clean mug. She glanced over her shoulder. "Did he even get you guys anything to drink?"

"He asked, then he kinda got excited about my omelet . . ." Sam hedged while Harry just chuckled.

"Water for her and I'll take a cup o' joe." Harry placed their order. "Mac's gettin' damn old and forgetful." He deliberately raised the tenor of his voice so Mac would hear him over the clatter of flatware on plates and the hum of the other customers' conversations.

"I heard that, you old so-and-so." Mac glared out at Harry over the pass-through.

"I meant for you to." Harry just grinned.

She and Megan chatted as Megan placed napkin-wrapped flatware at their places at the red Formica counter, rinsed some dirty plates and silverware, and rang up a departing customer's bill.

"'Scuse me, Madam Mayor." Butter sizzled as Max poured rich yellow eggs into a skillet and hollered through the open pass-through. "You need a hairnet and an apron if you intend to serve customers. You trying to get me busted by the health department?"

"Where's Sheila?" Megan scanned the diner as she dried her hands on a tea towel.

"Dentist. She has an abscess, I think." In the kitchen, Mac whipped eggs and poured them into a hot pan with great panache while Sam looked on in amazement. "We're at the slow time of the morning, so I sent her over to Doc Stanton."

Sam had never mastered the art of making an omelet. Hers always fell apart. She rose from her stool and paid close attention as Mac whisked frothy eggs in the well-buttered skillet, making sure all the mixture touched the hot pan. When it was almost all cooked, he added cheese, fresh spinach, and mushrooms and folded one side carefully. Then he hit the skillet handle with his palm while tilting the pan up, so the omelet flipped up onto itself, making a perfect cheesy delight. So that was the trick! She watched in awe as he held the plate up by the skillet and simply slid the eggy concoction onto it.

Megan sighed. "I'm not really here to work, Dad. I just stopped by when I saw Sam sitting in here. I'm on my way to a luncheon meeting with the arts council."

Mac barked a laugh. "You better eat something before you go. They'll serve you a tablespoon of dry chicken salad on a stale croissant with a few limp pieces of lettuce and call it lunch." He set two plates on the pass-through and pointed to the one on the right. "Harry"—he pointed to the other plate—"Sam."

"I'm glad I ran into you again, Sam." Megan placed the plates on the counter in front of them. "I wanted to invite you to the Christmas tree lighting on the square. It's Friday night. Will you still be here?"

Sam nearly went into a paroxysm of joy as she inhaled the scent of the herbed omelet Mac had plated up along with a few slices of fresh strawberries on the side, and a toasted baguette smeared with truffle butter. The distinct fragrance of basil and . . . was that thyme . . . wafted up. She met Megan's gaze over the plate and blinked. "Um . . . yes, I think I'll be here. I already sorta told Ali Flaherty I'd come to hear her sing, but thanks for a special invitation from the mayor."

"My pleasure. Enjoy the omelet." Megan grinned as she

leaned into the pass-through. "Dad, I'm outta here. You okay? Who's covering lunch?"

"Norma's coming in at eleven, so she should be here any minute, and Calvin just got here. He's out back. I'm all good." Mac came around to hug his daughter, while Sam hummed in pleasure as she took a second, then a third bite of her eggs.

"Amazing eggs, Mac." Sam lifted her fork in salute.

"I know." Mac folded his arms over his chest and leaned against the sink behind the counter. "It's what I do. How do you like the truffle butter?"

Sam swallowed a bite of toast. "I love it. I tried to make it at home once after I had it in France, but it just didn't taste the same. Yours tastes like Paris."

Mac nodded. "The secret is adding some finely chopped summer truffles to the butter along with the white truffle oil and salt. Also refrigerate it for a full day and let it soften to room temperature before you serve it."

"It's fabulous." She took another bite and closed her eyes in ecstasy. When she looked up from her plate, Harry was eyeing her, a big grin on his leathery face. She finished the bite. "What?"

"Nothing. I just love to see a woman who really enjoys good food." Harry dug into his own delicious-looking omelet.

"So do I." A husky voice behind her sent a shiver up her spine and Conor Flaherty strolled into the diner.

Chapter Ten

THE SUN SLANTING through the window of Mac's Riverside Diner caught Sam's auburn hair at just the right angle, creating a reddish-gold aura around her head. Conor opened the door quietly, wanting to take in the rightness of the scene before him—his good friends and this newcomer who was already turning his heart inside out. A storm of emotions whirled in him. Anxiety. Eagerness. Dread. Excitement. For the first time in two long years, he let himself feel it all. Everything. And it was eighth grade all over again—the moment when he saw Emmy in front of the band room and his heart had jumped with the same exact rush of feelings, except this time, the sensation wasn't foreign. It was familiar because this time he'd already known attraction so intense it set him back on his heels.

This wasn't love; he wasn't foolish enough to think he was falling in love with Sam Hayes, but the possibility was there and that was the biggest surprise. Not that it was happening so fast. No, that was Conor's way—he always jumped in feet first. The shock was that it had occurred at all. He'd truly believed losing Emmy had left his heart in so many pieces, it could never be put right again.

"Dude, get that look off your face before she turns around," Megan whispered as she passed him in the doorway.

Conor raised one brow, trying to look innocent, and Megan just gave him a pitying glance, shook her head, and patted his arm before she let the glass door shut behind her.

Sam was chatting with Mac and Harry between bites of what looked like an omelet and white truffle butter toast, which was actually the original reason he'd come by the diner in the first place. He'd missed Truffle Butter Tuesdays and it had been too long. He and Emmy had hit the diner regularly for Mac's amazing baguettes and butter. Besides, the diner was sort of on the way home from preschool . . . if he took the long way and drove along the river instead of back up the hill.

He'd already stopped by the bank and the hardware store and the riverside tasting room, where he'd replaced the burned-out spotlight over the parking lot. He caught himself hurrying through that task to avoid running into Charlotte. He just wasn't up for the awkwardness that had come between them since the lawsuit. And, okay, yes, he was hoping he'd run into Sam somewhere between Serendipity and Harry's office.

Clearly, she was enjoying her meal. He glanced at the vintage rooster clock above the pass-through—early for lunch and he couldn't believe she hadn't had breakfast at the

B&B. Rose never let anyone leave without at least a muffin and coffee. On the other hand, no one left Mac's with an empty stomach either, and Conor was sure Harry had insisted she order because he was giving her the same look of approval he'd given Conor last night when he'd gone back for a second helping of potato soup. Harry did love to see people enjoying good food.

She spun around on the stool when he seconded Harry's statement, her brown eyes wide and her cheeks pinkening adorably. She swallowed and smiled. "Hey, Conor."

"Hi, Sam."

Brilliant reply, Con. Eighth grade all over again?

He offered her a smile before nodding at Mac in an effort to regain his composure. Mac's look of astonished delight warmed his heart. He hadn't been into the diner for Truffle Butter Tuesday in ages. Two years, two months, and six days to be exact.

"Conor, great to see you! You're just in time. Got a loaf of French bread coming out of the oven in"—Mac pulled his long body up straight and peered over the pass-through— "fifty-four seconds." Grinning, he loped to the kitchen, whistling under his breath.

Conor slid onto the stool next to Sam, inhaling a tempting array of aromas—coffee, hot bread, basil, thyme, and the enticing citrus fragrance that was peculiar to Sam Hayes. She smelled like . . . like sunshine. He wanted to simply bask in the scent of her, but figured he'd be better served by returning her smile.

"Hello." He peered around her to acknowledge his old friend. "Harry."

"What're you doing in here?" Harry gave him a chin lift and took another bite of his baguette.

"It's Tuesday. That's why I'm here."

Harry snorted. "Sure, you just keep telling yourself that."

Conor leaned his elbows back on the counter, stuck his legs out in front of him, and eyed Sam's nearly empty plate. "What'd Mac serve up with your truffle butter toast?"

She chuckled. "So this really is a *thing* in this town? Truffle Butter Tuesday?"

"You bet." His hair flopped onto his forehead as he nodded and he shoved it back with his fingers. "Mac won't retail the stuff and he guards the recipe with his very life, so we all have to show up here on Tuesdays to eat our fill."

"Really? 'Cause he just gave—" Sam jerked, then snapped her lips closed and glared at Harry, who was sipping coffee and staring off into space. Clearing her throat, she started again. "He just gave me the most delicious omelet I've ever tasted. I'm officially a fan of Truffle Butter Tuesdays." She rubbed her side and gave Harry the stink eye.

What was that all about?

Conor shrugged as Mac set a plate in front of him, piled high with cheesy scrambled eggs, berries, and a baguette slathered in truffle butter. His buddy, the chef, had remembered his usual fare after all this time. Once again to his immense surprise, Conor was starving. Even though he cooked for Ali every morning, a bowl of cold cereal for breakfast wasn't going to cut it anymore. He tucked into the food with gusto. Damn, it felt good to be hungry again. And to sit next to Sam, who'd finished the last of her omelet and was resting her chin in her palm and gazing at him.

"No fancy omelet?" She nodded her head slightly toward his plate.

"Nope." Conor shoveled another bite of eggs onto his toast, chewed, and swallowed before he elaborated. "I just like eggs and cheese—no other stuff. Except bacon. I do love bacon."

"Bacon is a gift from heaven." Sam's eyes sparkled and Conor made a decision.

"Listen, if you're really planning to come up to the winery after Ali gets home from preschool, would you like to stay for supper? I'll make BLTs."

Sam set her napkin on her plate, and when she turned her stool around, their knees bumped, sending an electric zing through Conor's whole system.

"Thanks, I'd like that. See you sixish?" she said as she rose to leave.

However, unless he was rustier at this whole man/woman thing than he thought, her eyes said much more.

But she merely added, "Thanks for breakfast, Harry." And then she was on her way as he watched, his gut tightening at the easy sway of her hips.

"Something's woke you up, kid." Harry observed wryly after the door had closed behind Sam. "And I think it just walked out that door."

Conor piled the last of his eggs onto a sliver of toast and popped it in his mouth. An interesting way for Harry to put it because that was exactly how he felt—*awakened*. The fog of grief had lifted in the past few days and Conor was seeing life clearly again. He'd forgotten how much he enjoyed the fellowship at Mac's and lunches with Harry. He hadn't really paid attention to the bustle of River's Edge's holiday preparations since Emmy's death; but this morning, walking from the tasting room to the diner, his spirits had lifted at the sight of garland-wrapped light posts and old Noah Barker dressed as Santa, ringing the bell out in front of his hardware store. He exchanged greetings with sisters Dot and Mary Higgins as they hung a holly swag over the door of their quilt shop, and he peeked at the display of vintage Christmas ornaments on the tree in the window of Antiques and Uniques. Clyde Schwimmer, who was putting a star on the top of the tree, had tossed him a friendly, surprised smile when Conor passed.

"Just getting into the holiday spirit." Conor took a long drink of coffee. "How'd it go with Sam?"

"I think she's hoping Char will change her mind before we get to the hearing next week."

"I wouldn't count on that. I saw a sleek-looking Lotus pull into Char's drive as I was leaving this morning."

"Robert or Sabrina?" Harry tipped his head and gazed at him over the top of his wire-framed glasses.

"I'm pretty sure it was Rob." Conor rolled his eyes. His stepbrother was under the impression that cars were disposable. Seemed like he had a new one every time he showed up in River's Edge. Summers, he cruised around on a Harley, which Conor was certain upped Rob's opinion of his own cool factor immeasurably.

"Wonder what he's in town for," Harry mused, worrying his lower lip with his teeth.

"Probably here to make sure his mom is still on track," Conor replied.

Both of Charlotte's children had been checking in regularly since Donal's death, putting on quite a show of how lovingly they were looking after their widowed mother. Charlotte's demeanor changed after their visits; his normally sunny stepmother seemed closed and disheartened rather than cheered by her children's concern. He knew the pain of losing a spouse, and when Donal first passed, he and Charlotte had shared numerous nights of wine and commiseration. They'd grown closer in those weeks than they'd ever been before and she seemed grateful for his empathy.

Lately though, she'd withdrawn from all the Flahertys except for Ali, whom she almost seemed to cling to. The distance between Conor and his stepmother grew wider with each visit from Rob and Sabrina, so that by the time

Thanksgiving came around, Charlotte had opted to eat turkey with her twins at a hotel buffet in Cincinnati rather than share the holiday with the Flaherty brothers.

"I've tried talking to her." Harry shook his head. "She's so afraid of ticking off her kids, she can't listen to reason."

"I appreciate you trying, Harry." Conor sighed and spun around on the stool to stare out the picture window. "Sam's got lots of ammunition. I don't see how Char can win this one, but I hate what it's doing to us. She and Da were so happy together and we all love her."

"I know, kid. This stinks on ice," Harry agreed, turning on his stool to rest his elbows on the counter and gaze out at the holiday decorating bustle going on in the street outside. "Hey, Mac, you gonna put up that ratty silver tree again this year?"

"Are you trashing my vintage aluminum Christmas tree with the rotating color wheel?" Mac played it with just enough indignation, much to Harry's obvious delight.

"You need to move into the twenty-first century." Harry grinned at Conor, who was relishing the exchange. It had been too long since he'd heard Harry and Mac wrangle, and he'd missed their good-natured teasing.

"This is a retro diner, you old fart." Mac came out to gather up their plates and bus tables in the diner. "The aluminum tree is part of the ambiance. It stays. As a matter of fact"—he gave Conor a knowing wink—"I'm seriously considering hanging up Mom's old Styrofoam and plastic mistletoe ball . . . right about there." He pointed to the ceiling just in front of the door. "Might be fun to see how many customers notice it and take advantage." He brought the heavy dishpan full of dirty dishes around the counter and set it near the sink.

Conor couldn't help smiling, thinking about the mistletoe hanging in the winery and the kisses that had set his heart racing and a certain auburn-haired beauty who touched his cheek and left, her dark eyes full of promise as well as a hint of sadness. He wasn't sure what the promise was, or the sadness for that matter, but he intended to find out tonight.

"You'd take advantage of it, wouldn't you, my boy? I mean, if the opportunity presented itself?" Mac held the coffeepot over Conor's cup and gave him another broad wink. "Warm-up?"

SAM WASN'T SURE which of the two houses on the winery property belonged to Conor and Ali, so she took a shot and pulled into the first driveway she came to. Lights shone in the window of the roomy-looking ranch house and there was a pink tricycle on the porch. This must be the place.

The air was crisp and cold and the sun had begun to set over the hills, making a fiery, almost eerie, backdrop for the skeletal vineyards. Except for a few stray leaves that still clung to the now-dormant plants, the vines had been tucked in for the winter. She paused for a moment by her car, taking in the beautiful scene before her, soaking up the peaceful atmosphere of the sleeping vineyard, so different from the bustle of Chicago.

She hadn't missed the city at all since she'd been in River's Edge, even though she loved Chicago. Macy's windows were already dressed for Christmas and the huge Grand Tree was probably up and decorated in the rotunda at the Museum of Science and Industry. The Magnificent Mile was surely preparing for the Festival of Lights and the Christkindlmarket in Daley Plaza had been in full swing since before Thanksgiving.

Year before last, she'd dragged her mother and a reluctant David to the tree lighting at Millennium Park. The two of them groused so much about the crowds and the cold that she'd put them in a cab and sent them to Remington's, where they enjoyed martinis and appetizers and no doubt, an hour of dismissive speculation about what she was doing out among the great unwashed of Chicago.

She, on the other hand, had been soaking in the holiday spirit of carols sung by school choirs, of the aromas of pine, mulled cider, and hot pretzels, of millions of twinkling lights and the laughter and excited chatter of the crowd. She'd oohed and aahed with the others when the giant tree was lit and sang softly when the emcee invited everyone to join in a chorus of "Oh, Tannenbaum." She'd gotten a little misty when the children sang "Away in a Manger" and was grateful neither her mother nor David was there to witness her wiping her eyes. Last year, she simply went to the festivities on her own. It was easier that way.

Just then, a sports car pulled in behind her—a shiny, black Lotus Esprit—and a slender, blond-haired man stepped out and asked, "Can I help you?" His eyes raked over her in a glance so dismissive it completely contradicted his gracious question. He balanced a pizza box on one palm, shoved the car door shut with his hip, and ambled toward her.

"I must be at the wrong house."

"Who are you looking for?" The man's voice was gravelly, a smoker's voice, and when he drew closer, she could smell cigars on him. What a shame to ruin that gorgeous vehicle with cigar smoke. Hopefully, he wasn't actually smoking them in the car.

"Conor Flaherty. Am I at the right house?"

"No. His is the log house on the other side of the north vineyard. He's actually up at the barn though. I can see his car in the parking lot." He jerked his head in the general direction of the winery. His gray eyes shone with curiosity, and he looked vaguely familiar.

Suddenly, she realized why—he looked like Charlotte. This had to be Conor's stepbrother. "I'm Sam, a friend of Conor's." She extended her hand with a smile. "And you are?"

He ignored her gesture and instead gazed at her through

half-closed eyelids. "I know who you are, Ms. Hayes. I googled you after Mom told me you showed up last night at Conor's party."

She opened her mouth to defend herself, then thought better of it as he continued in the same contemptuous tone, "Sean sent you down here because that old fart Evans is too decrepit to handle our, I mean Mom's, contest of Donal's will." His eyes darkened and he closed the space between them just enough to appear menacing. "Don't think you can intimidate her into dropping the suit. She's earned a stake in this damn place. She worked her ass off for twelve years."

Sam drew in a deep breath and opened her car door, forcing Rob to step away. "If you know who I am, then you must know that I'm not at liberty to discuss this case with you. Good night, Mr. Pearson." She slid into her car and pulled the door shut, praying she hadn't overplayed her hand by revealing she knew his last name.

Rob stayed in the driveway, staring at her as she pulled forward into the wide space in front of the garage, turned around, and then very deliberately drove so close to the Lotus that her side mirror nearly brushed his front fender as she left the driveway.

Jerk. She hoped he was cringing.

Sam drove slowly up to the winery, fuming slightly over her encounter with Charlotte's son. He really was a snot; Harry wasn't kidding about that. But Harry's opinion hadn't prejudiced her against Rob Pearson. Rob had done that himself with the way he'd dismissed her like an annoying fly. Imagining him being friends with either of the kind and gentlemanly Flaherty brothers she was acquainted with was impossible. If what she saw of Rob was who he truly was, little wonder Donal played hell blending the two families.

She pushed down her irritation when she saw Ali, bundled up in her pink winter jacket, peering through the slats of the high deck that surrounded the winery building. The little girl squealed with delight when Sam got out of her car.

"Hey, Sam! Up here!" Ali waved vigorously, the pompom on her pink knit cap bobbling on her head.

"Hi, sweetie!" Ali's adorable smile caused the last vestiges of Sam's frustration to fall away, although she wanted to be sure to let Conor know that Rob and Charlotte knew who she was and why she was there. A frisson of disappointment went through her; Conor would no longer have a reason to pretend they were in a relationship. However, they'd been alone last night, so the delectable kisses under the mistletoe hadn't been for anyone else's benefit but his . . . and hers.

"Ali, get off the railing!" The man in question stood in the open doorway, dressed in khakis and a forest-green half-zip fleece sweater over a waffle-weave knit shirt. His too-long hair was tousled as though he'd been running his fingers through it, a pair of horn-rimmed glasses were shoved up on his head, and a couple of days' worth of stubble darkened his cheeks.

She stopped at the bottom of the stairs, her heart pounding. Did he have any idea how sexy he was?

He strode across the deck and swooped a giggling Ali up into his arms before turning to Sam with a shy smile. "Hey!"

No, he didn't have any idea, and somehow, that made him all the sexier.

Chapter Eleven

SAM WAS A little surprised that Conor served their supper in the tasting room until he pointed out, quite reasonably, that was where Zin and Merlot lived. It had taken almost an hour to find the shy kitty, but once they'd coaxed her out of hiding among the racks of wine, Sam had discovered that the little critter really did have freckles. She also had the loudest purr Sam had ever heard. When Merlot finally settled into Sam's lap and allowed her to stroke her soft fur, the little cat rumbled and vibrated like a motor.

"Did you have kitties when you were a little girl?" Ali asked as she teased Zin, the bigger cat, with a toy mouse on a string.

"No. My mother didn't like animals much," Sam said. "And when I spent summers at my Aunt Bette's house in northern Indiana, she didn't have kitties, either, because she was allergic to cats. But she did have a very grumpy old English bulldog with droopy ears and a bad attitude. He didn't like kids very much, and he only wanted to eat and sleep."

Ali furrowed her brow. "What does an English bulldog

look like?"

"Like this." Conor dropped gracefully next to Sam, stuck out his lower jaw, and made a snapping motion over his top lip with his teeth, then growled, which sent Ali into a giggling fit. He reached over to pet Merlot and his fingers stroked across Sam's on the cat's belly. When she instinctively started to draw her hand away, he increased the pressure and laced his fingers with hers for the briefest moment before releasing her and reaching out to pull Ali into his lap for tickles and kisses.

Ali settled into her father's lap and gazed at Sam, suddenly becoming very serious. "We had a yellow dog named Cooper, but he went to be with *Daideó* and my mommy in heaven."

Conor dropped a kiss on the top of Ali's dark head before resting his chin there. "*Daideó* is Irish for Grandfather—my dad," he explained. "Cooper was a golden retriever who actually belonged to Da, but he lived in uneasy truce here at the cellar with these two." He indicated the cats who were vying for position in Sam's lap.

"Da says we can get a new dog when I'm old enough to feed it and clean up after it myself." Ali went into a long explanation of what kind of dog she wanted, while Sam stroked the cats and watched through half-closed eyes as Conor rubbed his cheek on his daughter's hair.

Pets were not a thing in the luxury high-rise apartment on Chicago's Gold Coast where Sam had been raised. Her mother had a strong distaste for cats and dogs, which was rather surprising since she'd grown up on a rural Illinois farm. But when Carlynne Waters came to the big city and met and married up-and-coming attorney, Griffin Hayes, the farm became a distant memory.

Sam never knew her grandparents and had been to the farm only once—when the property was put up for sale, right after her grandmother and grandfather died in a fire that destroyed the farmhouse. She remembered a bulldozer scraping the charred remains of the house into a pile, an old barn filled with rusty equipment, and an ancient pickup truck sitting among the weeds in the yard. The place frightened ten-year-old Samantha, and her mother hadn't helped when she jerked Sam away from a gray kitten that was cowering under the pickup.

"Leave it alone!" she'd scolded. "God only knows what kind of vermin it's carrying." Then Carlynne had grasped Sam's shoulders and said through clenched teeth, "See this? This is what happens when you don't strive to better yourself. To study hard and get a good education and *be* something. You end up like this." The contempt in her voice haunted Sam for ages—every time she considered skipping a class or winging a test.

But the little girl who'd longed to rescue the kitten came to the surface as she sat cross-legged on the floor of the winery, held Merlot, and laughed with Conor and Ali.

"JUST ONE MORE game, Da. Please?" Ali turned her mega-watt smile on Conor and he waffled.

They'd eaten delicious BLTs dressed with a secret sauce that Conor teasingly refused to share the recipe for. Sam had tasted carefully, trying to discern the ingredients, but he'd just chuckled and shook his head when she guessed. They played five rounds of Uno after Ali discovered, much to her astonishment, that Sam had never heard of the game. Sam was amazed at the skill with which the four-year-old strategized to win three of the five rounds. Conor won the first round and Sam had won the last one, pleased as punch she'd finally gotten the hang of the game.

"I want to win one more." Clearly Ali could see her dad was wavering. "Please, please?"

Conor glanced at his watch. "Nope. We're already past your bedtime."

"Awww . . ." Ali folded her arms across her chest and thrust out her lower lip.

"Don't you think it would be nice to end our time together with Sam's win since it's her first time to play?" Conor gathered up the red-and-black cards, straightened them, and shoved them back into their box.

"I guess." Ali pouted for a full ten seconds before her little face brightened. "Can Sam read me my bedtime story tonight?"

"That's entirely up to Sam."

"Sure, I'd love to read you a story." Sam rose from the tall table and took wineglasses and a sippy cup and rinsed them at the sink behind the tasting bar before gathering up her coat and purse. "Let me follow you over to your house, okay?"

THE TWO-STORY LOG house sprawled on the hillside not far from the winery. A covered porch wrapped around three sides with one side screened in. She parked behind Conor's SUV and wandered up the wide steps while he released Ali from her car seat and got the cooler containing the remains of supper from the back. Lights shone warm and inviting in the windows and the front door was a heavy wooden affair with an etched-glass panel in the center. Conor stepped past it and held the side screened porch door open with his hip while Ali, then Sam, scurried through.

A pair of lit sconces by the back door revealed dark wicker furniture with no cushions on them in the screened porch. Conor led them in and flipped a switch that bathed the roomy open kitchen in soft light. Sam drew in a breath. *What an amazing kitchen!* Fully gourmet with stainless-steel appliances, cherry cabinets, and granite surfaces throughout, the kitchen included a wide island that was the perfect spot to prep food. Immediately, she longed to cook something—

anything—on the professional-grade gas range or bake a pie in one of the double ovens. The stuccoed walls were painted soft yellow, and the room opened onto an intimate dining area and then to a high-ceilinged living room. "This is incredible, Conor."

Conor set the cooler on the floor by the island. "This was our dream kitchen. We both love to cook."

"It's beautiful." Sam wandered around, admiring the log walls in the living room and the fieldstone fireplace that took up one whole end. The fact that he referred to both himself and his dead wife in the present tense wasn't lost on her, but she put it out of her mind. It had to be hard to stop using *us* and *we* after a spouse died.

"We gathered all the fireplace stones from fields and creeks around here and the mantel is a chunk of a hickory tree that Da took down by his place." Pride colored his tone.

Sam stared up at the vastness of the beamed ceiling and the stars shining in through the skylights. "This place is huge. Did you build it all yourself?"

"No, we had a log home company from Rising Sun come in and put up the house and do the roof, the fireplace, the porches, and the drywall. They finished the inside walls that we left as logs and we hired out the electrical and the plumbing, but we did all the rest of the inside work." He indicated with a sweep of his arms. "Painting, floors, and trim. It took us about six months, but we had good help. Aidan was still home and Sean and Bren drove down to help us on weekends. Even folks from town came up and lent a hand."

"Wow." She walked around the big leather sofa to look closer at the fireplace stones and mantel, where she noticed a candid picture of a lovely, petite blonde-haired woman in a white dress standing in a field of wild flowers and holding a wide-brimmed hat. Her hair was blowing in the breeze and the photographer had caught her just as she brushed it back with one small hand.

"That's Mommy." Ali had crept up next to Sam. "I didn't know her very well. She went to heaven when I was little."

Sam stared at the picture and felt, rather than saw, Conor come up behind her.

"Emmy," he said quietly.

When she glanced over her shoulder, his eyes were so soft it nearly took her breath away. Dear Lord in heaven, Conor Flaherty was still an *us*, in spite of the kiss under the mistletoe. In spite of his obvious attraction to her.

Looking around the room, she saw a couple more pictures of him and his wife on the end tables. They looked so blissfully happy together, her heart ached. Dismay and something else that felt a little like dread welled up in her, so she swallowed, forcing herself to focus on Ali, who was pointing and chattering.

"And that's *Daideó* and Grammy Char." She indicated another photo on the mantel and then another. "There's all of us from Christmas. Uncle Sean, Uncle Bren, Da *Daideó*,

Grammy Char, Uncle Aiden, and me in the middle with Cooper." She grinned up at Sam. "I'm bigger now."

"Yes, you are bigger." Conor picked his daughter up and swung her upside down so her hair nearly brushed the floor, while Ali giggled. "And you're getting chattier by the day, kiddo." He set her back down and turned her toward the staircase. "Get upstairs and get ready for bed. We'll be up in three minutes and Sam can read you a story. And please don't pick the longest story on your bookshelf."

"I already picked Fancy Nancy for tonight." Ali scampered off, still giggling. "Get ready, Sam, I have new pink footie jammies! They're so cool!"

STORYTIME WENT OFF without a hitch, with Conor appearing in the doorway just as they finished the last page of *Fancy Nancy Splendiferous Christmas*, a book that delighted Sam just as much as it did Ali. While Conor switched on a green turtle nightlight that projected stars and the moon on Ali's ceiling and said final good nights to his daughter, Sam headed down the hall, but stopped on the landing to peer at the gallery of family pictures in the stairwell. She scrutinized each photo—probably at least thirty of them chronicling the timeline of Conor's life with Emmy. It was all there.

A collage of their dating years, starting with, according to the banner over their heads, a dance at River's Edge Junior

High School and going right up through their college graduation day. Sam's heart dropped. These two had been together forever. They were soul mates. And why did that bother her so much? It wasn't like she and Conor were involved. She shook her head and continued down the row of photographs.

A large wedding portrait took center stage with an angelic Emmy in a cream-colored lace gown and Conor looking gorgeous, but a little dorky, in a billowy white shirt and black pants. Sam recognized the gazebo in the vineyard as the setting. Honeymoon shots from what looked like the California wine country, and a photo of Conor carrying his bride over the threshold of their new log home. Above those, one of Emmy rosy-cheeked and round with Conor grinning behind her, his hands on her belly. Then the inevitable new-parent shot of the two of them in the delivery room beaming like fools over a newborn Alannah. Conor, in scrubs, looking like the king of the world and Emmy, a blonde and perfect earth mother.

At last she came to a poignant black-and-white photograph of Ali and Emmy reading together on Emmy's hospital bed. They appeared almost ethereal in the sunlight that streamed through the window and over the bed. She could only see half of Emmy's face, but her head was swathed in a bright scarf, and the arms she had wrapped around Ali were thin and pale. Staring at the photo, Sam's throat tightened as she clenched her fingers together and pressed them against her lips.

"That was taken about a week or so before she died." Conor sat on the stair several steps above the landing and leaned back on his elbows. "Ali thinks she remembers the day, but I think she really just has that picture in her head."

Sam dropped her hands, overwhelmed by the photos, by the little girl sleeping upstairs, by the beautiful house . . . by the sheer *Emmy* of it all. And then there was the man sitting on the stairs eyeing her. She had no idea what to say to him. But when she looked into his face, she was surprised. He wasn't closed up. She didn't see sorrow or regret or anger or any of the emotions she expected to see in his expression. Instead, he was open, smiling an enigmatic little smile that seemed like an invitation.

"Conor," she breathed. "Will you tell me about Emmy?"

Chapter Twelve

C ONOR DIDN'T THINK he could be any more attracted to Sam, but once again, her words touched a place in him he thought was dead forever.

How does she do that?

Sam extended her hand and every nerve in his body jangled as she led him down the stairs to the living room. She was going to have to drive again so he decided against pouring more wine. Instead, he turned on the gas fire, yanked his fleece jacket over his head, and tossed it on the club chair. Between the fire and well . . . Sam, the fleece would be too hot. They settled on the leather sofa—the sofa that Emmy had capitulated on when they built the house. She'd wanted chintz, but Conor just couldn't do the English garden thing in his log living room. So they'd compromised, leather here and chintz in their bedroom, which was still painted soft sage green. Charlotte had brought him a more masculine duvet cover and shams and tucked the flowered bed linens in the closet not long after Emmy's memorial service. It struck him that he'd never thanked her for that small kindness.

His mind was reeling when Sam put about a foot of space between them, kicked off her shoes, and curled her long legs under her. She turned to face him in the firelight that lent an air of intimacy to the vast space. Her auburn hair escaped from the bun on the top of her head and tendrils curled around her ears and cheeks. Conor longed to release it and tangle his fingers in the red-gold strands.

She tilted her head and offered him a smile. "Talk to me, Conor. From what I've seen here, she was an extraordinary woman."

Extraordinary. Not the word he would've chosen for his darling Emmy because she was, frankly, the most ordinary of women, which was what he loved best about her. Her simple beauty, her warm, friendly nature, her easy laughter that bubbled over at the least provocation—wildflowers on the ridge above the winery, the sun sparkling on the Ohio, new green shoots in her vegetable garden as May turned to June, the little ones in her kindergarten classes, and most of all, her utter joy in him and Ali.

He began to speak, slowly at first and then more openly as Sam's smile widened. "She was the light of my life."

He told her about meeting Emmy in eighth grade and falling in love with her in the mere moments it took him to traverse the band hall. His heart nearly burst when Sam chuckled delightedly at his *Say Anything* moment one night in high school after he and Emmy had argued over him not being willing to be on the homecoming court with her.

Conor could tell Sam was picturing him serenading Emmy while holding a boom box over his head.

"What did you sing?" she asked, her brown eyes sparkling with curiosity as she leaned toward him.

God, she really wants to know.

He shrugged as heat rose in his cheeks. "I don't remember."

"You do, too." She pointed at him. "Come on, tell me."

"Okay, it was an old Beatles tune, 'And I Love Her.'" He ducked his head, unable to meet her gaze. "So sappy. I got the cassette tape from Da's collection, borrowed his old boom box, and memorized it in an afternoon while I was nursing my broken heart."

"Did it work?"

"It did." He nodded and grinned at the memory of Emmy hanging out of her upstairs bedroom window, her long blonde hair shimmering in the moonlight. "She never let me forget it, though. She chose it as the song we danced to at our wedding, and of course, she had the DJ tell the story about the big nerd she was marrying."

When Sam threw her head back and chortled, he suddenly realized that although he was talking about Emmy, there was no stabbing pain in his chest, no sorrow filling his heart and head. Just warm, funny memories that he *wanted* to share with this incredible woman.

He talked and then talked some more, spilling his whole story, all about how excited they'd been when they found out

Emmy was pregnant and how terrified when pain sent her back to the doctor and they found the tumors. His throat tightened only slightly and he stared at the fire as he talked about Emmy's determination to do nothing about the cancer until after Ali was born and how the tumors had metastasized as their baby had grown in her belly. After Ali's birth, a few rounds of chemo eased the pain, but it was too late.

"Oh, Conor." Sam's voice was husky, and when he looked up, tears shimmered in her eyes. She pressed her hands to her chest. "I'm so terribly sorry. How do you ever . . ." Her voice broke.

He was so taken aback by the sincerity of her sympathy that he just stared at her for a moment. "You learn to go on. You have no choice. But there's always a hole in you," he said finally and then cursed his damn honesty when Sam increased infinitesimally the space between them on the sofa.

SAM BLINKED BACK the tears that threatened to spill over as she shifted slightly on the buttery leather couch. Her heart ached. What was it like to love and be loved so thoroughly? She pulled her gaze away from his and watched the gas flames dance in the fireplace. Her parents certainly hadn't had the kind of marriage Conor described—not even close. They'd lived separate lives for all of Sam's growing-up years; social-climbing Carlynne had little time for a husband or child and had basically turned Sam over to Griffin and the nanny.

Aunt Bette had never been married, although she had a "gentleman friend"—an artist who lived in Arizona whom she saw several times a year. Sam had met Joe Samuels and knew the loving bond he and Bette shared; however, they both lived their own lives and as far as she knew, neither of them had any interest in changing their unconventional relationship.

"I've never known that kind of love," she admitted, not meeting Conor's intense gaze.

"Never?" Doubt colored his tone.

"Well . . ." She hesitated, unsure whether it was appropriate to be sharing so much intimate information with a man she'd only known for a few days. Yet he had told his story, and somehow, she felt like she'd known him forever. "There was Andy, my college boyfriend. I was crazy about him. Alas, it wasn't meant to be." She played it off with a touch of melodrama and a shrug, even though the fact was she'd loved that quirky musician with her whole being.

"What happened?" Conor moved closer to her on the couch, so close their thighs almost touched and she could sense the warmth of his body, smell his clean, woodsy scent.

The urge to scoot away did battle with the desire to throw herself into his arms and kiss him stupid. So she stayed and took a deep breath. "He was a drummer and he left school to tour Europe with a rock band. He's probably still playing small clubs in Munich or Paris for all I know. He never wrote or contacted me after he left. I kept hoping he'd send for me and back then, I would've gone." She kept it simple. The whole story was still a bit painful to tell, although nothing in her ordinary life could possibly compare to the anguish Conor had suffered. She felt foolish for even trying to explain the heartbreak of Andy's abrupt departure from her life, but even at the tender age of twenty-one, it had hardened her enough that she'd kept a cool distance in her other relationships after that, focusing instead on becoming the best divorce lawyer in Chicago.

"But not now?" Conor extended his arm along the back of the sofa and let his fingers toy with the hair that had loosened from her bun and curled over her collar.

Her heart had hurt so badly when Andy left, she'd steeled her will, deciding never to open herself up like that again. And she hadn't. Even her engagement to David had been more like a business relationship, orchestrated by her mother, who thought he was quite perfect. But now, the whisper touch of Conor's fingers on her neck had driven Andy's and David's images right out of her head . . . and heart.

"Not now." She shook her head and offered him a small smile. "I grew up."

"Do you like your life?" He asked the question so casually; it almost could've been *Do you like the weather in Chicago?* And he'd moved closer, so close, his breath warmed her cheek.

She gave him a cocktail-party answer without turning her head. "Chicago is great. I love snow and the lake. I was raised there, so it's my hometown. I have a great apartment near the lakeshore and summers are great because I can walk to the beach or go to the museums or to concerts at Navy Pier . . . It's a great place to live . . ." She was talking too fast, and seriously, how many times could a person use the word *great* in a sentence before it stops being believable? She shut her mouth and laced her fingers together in her lap, daring a sideways glance at him.

He wore the same enigmatic smile and his blue eyes smoldered as he watched and waited for her to answer the question he'd actually asked.

She gave it another try. "I love being an attorney." Her voice came out raspy. So she cleared her throat and started again, still not facing him because facing him meant their lips would be mere inches apart and more than anything, she wanted him to kiss her. "I've always wanted to be a lawyer. It was my greatest childhood wish to be just like my dad. He loved the law. He was a lawyer and a judge, and he was the best person I knew."

"You got your wish." Conor tipped his head forward, clearly trying to see into her eyes.

Sam stared at her hands. "I suppose I did."

"I'm sensing you're not delighted with your career at Stark, Randolph, Smith, and Flaherty."

Sam's heart pounded in her ears and she could barely breathe with Conor so close. Yet she wanted him closer and that confused her to the point she couldn't find the words to refute his observation, but she tried. "I'm not sure anymore." The words were out before she had a chance to stop them. "I do love the law—it's real and it's something I understand, but I don't know if I can be The Dragon Lady anymore. Not after—"

"The Dragon Lady?" Conor raised one brow.

"A silly nickname I was given by a reporter a couple of years ago because I wasn't letting these men tromp all over their wives, trading them in for younger women and abandoning their families. I fight so hard to protect them, but now after . . ."

"What happened, Samantha?"

When he said her full name in a husky voice so filled with concern, she swiped her cheeks and met his gaze. Without another moment of thought, she poured out the story of that dreadful night when Carter Briggs had rampaged through his ex-wife's house and murdered his family. From the depths of her soul, she found the words to tell him how hard it was to try to please everyone in her life, especially when none of the people she was trying to please were her. But then stupid, stupid tears pressed against her eyelids and she blinked them away, hoping he hadn't noticed.

But Conor's hand had drifted to her shoulder and he was gently pressing her to his broad chest. His lips were warm against her forehead as he tugged her bun free. He combed his fingers through her hair and murmured soft little comforts as she unclenched her hands and nestled into his embrace. Somehow, magically, it felt as though he already knew everything—the sadness at the loss of her father, the struggle to be what her mother wanted, the wrenching reality of dealing daily with broken marriages and broken lives. That was impossible of course; they barely knew each other. But, oh, how she wanted to know him! And, yes, for just a moment, she wanted to know what it was like to be Emmy . . . to be so loved and desired.

She tipped her head back and when she saw tenderness and her own hunger reflected in his blue, blue eyes, all clear thought fled. She slipped her hand up and pulled his face down to hers. The bristle of a couple of days' worth of scruff tickled her cheek as their lips met and Sam smiled into a kiss that turned her inside out. He kissed her softly, as if he cherished her—warm kisses that started out gentle, then swiftly became more.

When the kisses deepened and their mouths fused, Conor's tongue touched the seam of her lips, seeking entry. A shiver coursed through her as she opened to him and their tongues twined and danced for a moment. He pulled back to gaze at her. The wonder and desire in his eyes made her heart ache and sent white-hot heat to her core.

He pulled her over onto his lap as his lips found her cheek, her temple, and the ultra-sensitive skin in front her ear. She touched the stubble on his cheek and he pressed a kiss into her palm. She slid her hand down to his chest, amazed at the quick pace of his heart beneath the knit shirt. Resting her cheek on his shoulder, she breathed in the scent of him, while his hand smoothed down her spine and over her hip. Everywhere he touched, heat followed and when his fingers slipped under her sweater and bunched the fabric of her silk camisole, she nearly stopped breathing.

His mouth sought hers again, taking her lips fiercely, his tongue plunging in to meet hers as he shoved his fingers into her hair. His tongue tasted and stroked and explored her mouth and he took tiny nips of her lips. She met him stroke for stroke, tasting his wine-sweet breath and the flavors of bacon and chocolate on his tongue. Reaching her arms around his neck, she slid her fingers into the thick toffee-colored hair that fell over his collar. The man sure could kiss.

Sam drew her head back to take a breath and gazed at him. His hair was tousled, his eyes were almost navy in the dim light, and his smile was heart-stoppingly sexy. He closed his eyes for a second and dropped his head against the back of the sofa even as his fingers continued their sensual massage under her sweater. He made a groaning noise in the back of his throat that sent a shiver of longing through her. That same hot hunger burned in his eyes as he took her lips again and his hand moved urgently over her hip. Her heart pounded in her ears and—

His head popped up and he released her so quickly she

practically fell off his lap. Conor untangled himself from her arms, and when she scooted back onto the sofa, he stood, raking his fingers through his hair and blinking in confusion. Through the heated haze, her brain finally kicked back into gear. Someone was pounding on the front door.

Chapter Thirteen

C ONOR SHOOK HIS head and glanced at the clock above the fireplace. Who would be knocking on his door at ten o'clock at night? The winery was closed. They'd turned off the lights and locked all the doors when they left after supper. He canted his head, listening for the alarm over the insistent rapping on the heavy wooden door before glancing down at his phone on the table. Nothing. So not the alarm company.

He yanked his shirt down, hoping to hide the evidence of the moments of passion with Sam and with a wry smile in her direction, he headed for the door. "This better be a dire emergency or someone telling me I've just won a million bucks."

When she chuckled, he looked back over his shoulder and almost moaned at the sensual longing in her eyes. "Actually, forget the million. The only thing I could excuse for interrupting us right now is a dire—"

"Conor!" An urgent voice outside the door interrupted him.

Charlotte?

He ran the last few steps across the living room, quickly unlocked the door, and threw it open.

His stepmother stood shivering in the pool of light on the stoop, tears streaming down her face. "Oh, Conor! I need your help." She was wild-eyed and breathless and clad only in a sweater and jeans and a pair of canvas slip-ons. Her always-perfect hair was wind-tossed and mascara smudged dark circles under her eyes.

"Good Lord, Char, get in here!" He held the door wide as he reached for her hand. "Where's your coat? It's freezing out here."

As soon as he shut the door, Charlotte grasped his arm. "P-please, Conor. I need your help."

"Of course, Char, anything." He led her to the big leather chair where Sam had the afghan from the back of the couch waiting. He tossed her a grateful smile as she wrapped the knitted blanket around Char's shaking shoulders.

Sam sat on the big chest that served as a coffee table and took both of Char's hands in her own. "God, your hands are like ice. You need something hot. Tea or hot chocolate?" She jumped up and headed to the kitchen at the end of the vast open-concept living space. In spite of his concern for his stepmother, Conor couldn't help admiring Sam's elegant, long-limbed stride.

"T-tea, please." Charlotte pulled the afghan closer, before running her fingers through her hair in a weak attempt at straightening it.

Sam made herself right at home in his kitchen, finding the switch that flooded the room with bright light, filling the kettle that lived on the stove, and putting it on to heat. "Conor, you do have tea, right?" She gave him an utterly adorable lopsided grin over the bar that separated the cooking area from the rest of the room.

"I do. It's in the pantry—in the hall back there across from the laundry room." He took Sam's place on the wooden trunk that had once been his great-grandfather's tool chest and reached out to rub Charlotte's arms to try to bring some warmth back to her system.

Char leaned gratefully against him, her face hidden against his shoulder as he held her and let her cry it out. After a few minutes, she took a huge shuddering breath and fell back against the chair.

Sam appeared behind her with a damp washcloth and a hand towel—she'd apparently also found the half bath. "Here, take this and wipe your face." She offered it to Char, who gave her a weepy smile.

The kettle whistled and Sam scurried to heed its shrill beckoning. She was back with a mug of steaming tea by the time Char had pressed the washcloth to her face, wiped away most of the mascara, and dabbed with the towel. She looked a little better, although tears still shimmered in her gray eyes.

Sam took the towel and facecloth when Char was finished and placed them on the kitchen bar before taking her jacket from the hook by the door where Conor had hung it earlier. "I'm going to head out. This is clearly family business. You two don't need me here."

"Wait!" Charlotte raised the hand that wasn't holding the mug of tea. "Please stay."

Conor and Sam exchanged a wary glance over the older woman's head. His stomach tightened, but he shrugged, and he and Sam settled on opposite ends of the sofa, even though he would rather have had her snuggled up beside him.

"I know who you are." Char gave Sam a tremulous smile. "I know you're a lawyer from Sean's firm in Chicago and I know you're here to represent the boys in . . . in this stupid, stupid lawsuit." She stopped, her smile widened ever so slightly, and an unexpected twinkle appeared in her eyes. "Although from the guilty looks on both your faces when you opened the door, Con, my boy, I think what I interrupted just now was anything but lawyerly."

Conor's face felt hot and when he side-eyed Sam, a rosy flush had risen to her cheeks as well. Cripes, it was high school all over again.

Char chuckled in spite of the tears. "I'm delighted. You seem lovely, my dear, and it's high time Conor rejoined the human r-race." Her voice trembled and she blinked, her face sober again.

"Char, what's going on?" Conor reached for her hands. They were still ice cold.

"It's Rob and Sabrina, they—" She broke off, alarm taking over her expression once again and suddenly a rush of words poured out. "Oh, Conor, I don't want to sue you. I-I never wanted this. It was all Rob's idea. He and Sabrina believed I was getting a raw deal by being left out of the winery, and they convinced me to contest Donal's will, even though I knew this wasn't what he wanted. We'd talked about it. But . . . but the kids were . . . they made me think . . . and now—" Another storm of weeping interrupted her.

Conor nodded encouragement. What the hell were her kids up to? It seemed every time they turned up, poor Char was distressed. "What happened tonight?"

"I-I was in the k-kitchen cleaning up after supper. Rob brought pizza. E-everything was fine until he told me who Sam here was. He was irritated I hadn't figured that out when we trimmed the tree last night. But how . . . how could I know? Then I told him I didn't think I wanted to continue the suit and he was"—she stopped and swallowed hard—"he was furious. He was saying really horrible things, so finally I just told him fine, we'd let it be. I c-couldn't handle the ugliness." She rubbed her palms over her face. "After supper, I heard him talking in the living room, so I left the water running in the kitchen and tiptoed into the hall to listen." She put one hand on her chest and shook her head sadly. "Eavesdropping on my own son! This is who I've become, Conor." She pulled the blanket closer. "I hate it. I hate this. I hate all of it!"

"What'd you hear, Char?" Conor's heart pounded.

If those two idiots had done anything to hurt his step-mother, he was prepared to do battle. The poor woman was obviously distraught and dramatic wasn't her nature. Charlotte was pretty level-headed and sensible.

Her teeth worried her lower lip and she took another shuddering breath. "He told Sabrina if I ended the suit, they could have me declared incompetent and they'd have power of attorney over all my affairs. He said he knew a doctor who'd testify." She reached for Conor's hand and her grip was like iron. "I heard him tell her it would be easy to make me look like I was losing my mind. I do forget things now and again—doesn't everyone? God, I'm scared. I'm so scared."

SAM'S HEART DROPPED and for a moment, no one said a word as she and Conor tried to absorb what Charlotte was telling them. "Good God, Conor!" Sam gasped finally. "They're talking about gaslighting her!"

He and Char both gaped at her, confusion evident in their faces.

Sam explained quickly before either one of them could ask the question. "It's a reference from an old movie from the forties—*Gaslight*—where Charles Boyer tries to convince Ingrid Bergman she's crazy. I can't remember the exact story, something about him changing the brightness of the gaslights in their home and convincing her it's her imagination. He does other stuff too, but basically he makes her think she's delusional."

"They can't do that," Conor scoffed, then stared at her. "Can they?"

"Of course they can." Sam rose and paced in front of the fireplace, her mind working a mile a minute. "There was a case when I first joined the firm where a man was trying to get power of attorney over his father's estate. It got ugly because the father was perfectly competent. However the son was doing everything he could to prove otherwise."

"God, Conor! What am I going to do?" Charlotte released Conor's hand and scraped her fingers through her gray-blond hair. "I don't want to sue you boys. I love you all dearly. I'm so sorry. I never wanted to go against Donal's wishes. I let the kids convince me to do it. And now everything's completely out of hand."

Sam bit her lip. Technically, should she even be in on this conversation? Maybe they should call Sean for some guidance. But first, she had to pull Conor aside and let him know what she was thinking. She tapped his shoulder lightly. "Conor, you want to help me in the kitchen for a minute?"

He glanced up, then did a double-take when she widened her eyes. "Um, sure. Hold tight, Char. We'll get this figured out."

Sam led the way to the kitchen and kept her voice low. "We need to call Sean. She can drop the suit if she wants to, but if Rob finds her here, her kids will mostly likely immediately turn around and claim collusion. They'll say we influenced her, and voila, they'll have the first peg they need to hang their incompetence hat on."

"Do you have your phone?" He patted his pockets. "Mine's on the table in the living room."

"It's in my coat pocket." Sam slid around him to grab her phone, all the time keeping an eye on Char, shivering in the big chair by the fireplace.

Conor was peering anxiously out the window over the sink when she returned. "What if he tries to follow her? He's bound to show up here—her car's in the garage. Where else would she go?"

The knots in Sam's stomach tightened as she scrolled through her contacts for Sean's number. Shaking her head, she tried to compose her rioting thoughts while it rang through. "Sean? It's Sam." She spoke as softly as she could and moved to the back door to avoid Charlotte overhearing.

"Hey, Sam, how's it going down there? My little brother behaving himself?" Sean's hearty voice was loud enough that Conor cringed and pointed to the powder room by the back door. He opened a cupboard below the bar and grabbed a bottle of whiskey, indicating with a hand signal his intention to return to his stepmother.

Sam slipped into the half bath and shut the door, praying she'd keep her cell signal. "We've got a bit of an issue."

"Yeah?" She heard him take a sip of a beverage and could

picture Sean's handsome face, one brow quirked.

"I'm at Conor's and Charlotte just showed up here . . ." Sam began and then went on to explain the events of the last few minutes. After the shortest version she could muster, she asked, "What do you think?"

Sean didn't hesitate. "I think it's great she wants to drop the suit, but you need to get her out of there before Rob comes looking for her."

"Ethically, what can *I* do here?" Sam chewed her lower lip. "I feel like I need to just get the heck out before her son shows up. I don't want him accusing Conor and me of undue influence. If he does, that's just going to fuel his fire to have her declared incompetent."

"Well, I can attest there's nothing incompetent about our Char. Hell, she's sharp as a tack. Those two have just scared her to death." Sam could hear the disgust in his tone loud and clear.

"What do you want me to do?"

"Have Conor call Teresa Ashton and ask her to come pick up Char." He exhaled deeply. "And let me talk to Conor for a minute. He needs to tell Char that if she's serious about dropping the suit, then she should call that shyster in Louisville and let him know. In the meantime, you phone Harry and have him meet Char at Teresa and Frank's. She's going to need him to draw up a motion for dismissal. I'm sure the guy her kids hired is going to try to talk her out of dropping the contest. Harry can help her navigate that."

"Okay." Tension began to release in Sam's shoulders and spine. "Give me five minutes to get on my way, then you call Conor on his cell. I've got Harry's card. I'll call him when I get in the car." She hesitated. "And thanks, Sean. I-I wasn't positive what direction to head here. First time anyone's ever dropped a suit against one of my clients."

"You're doing fine, kid." Sam heard his smile and she breathed a small sigh of relief. "Your instincts to stay out of the fray are right on target. Rob and Sabrina can't possibly accuse you of any collusion. Tell Conor I'll call him, and he and I can talk to Char together. Oh, and Sam, nice work. Thank you."

"I didn't do anything." Sam saw her own wry smile reflected in the mirror above the vanity. "Her kids sorta pooped in their own nest when they started plotting tonight."

"Yeah, those two have never respected Char's strength of character, which is mostly her own doing because she's constantly given in to them about everything. I'm glad she's finally growing a backbone. About freakin' time."

"I'm going to get out of here. I'll call Harry and probably head back up to Chicago in the morning."

"Why don't you stay a few days?" Sean said, almost too casually. "That little town puts on quite a Christmas display. I think Ali's preschool class is singing at the tree-lighting ceremony this weekend."

"I'll see." Sam furrowed her brow. Her heart ached. She

wanted nothing more than to stay in River's Edge. To see Ali sing at the tree lighting. To stand beside Conor in the chilly, starry night while the town lit up for the holidays. But, the longer she stayed, the harder it would be to go and she had to go.

Didn't she?

Chapter Fourteen

CONOR EYED SAM as she gathered up her belongings, pulled on her coat, and wrapped her brightly colored scarf around her throat. Sighing, he tossed a glance at Char before striding to Sam. "Don't go," he whispered.

"I have to." She touched his face. "Ethically, I can't be here right now."

His shoulders drooped. "I know." For some reason it felt like she was leaving forever. "I'll see you tomorrow?"

She gave him a regretful look as his phone chimed on the coffee table and he expelled a frustrated breath. "Go answer that. It's Sean. He'll tell you what to do. I'll talk to you tomorrow. Lock this door, okay?" She pressed her lips to his for an instant, then scooted out the door on a rush of chilly night air.

"Hey, Bro." Sean's voice boomed over the phone so loud that Conor held the device away from his ear and messed with the screen to lower the volume. He'd forgotten to turn it down after he and Ali had Skyped with Emmy's parents in San Diego after school earlier in the day. "Is Sam outta there?"

"Yeah, she's gone. Sean, help." Conor had no problem confessing how jumbled his thoughts were at this point. Leftover hunger for Sam's kisses melded with concern for Charlotte and confusion about how to handle her latest revelation. Plus, he was more than a little worried about Rob showing up. He surely did not want a scene with his stepbrother. He had no problem imagining Rob storming the house, his blustery outburst waking Ali and frightening her.

Sean's deep voice soothed some of the anxiety. "Okay, listen. Call Teresa and have her pick up Charlotte. We need to keep her away from Rob, but we also need her out of your house or Rob and Sabrina will start screaming undue influence. Sam's going to call Harry and have him meet Char at Frank and Teresa's."

"Okay." Conor sat down on the sofa, reached for Charlotte's shaking hand, and gave it a squeeze.

"How's she doing?" Sean's tone was laced with worry.

"She's doing okay." Conor tipped his head to peer into Char's eyes. She certainly seemed calmer. "We gave her tea and wrapped her up in a blanket."

"Does she have her phone?"

"I dunno. Char, do you have your phone with you?"

"Yes." Charlotte set her cup of tea on the table beside the chair and reached into the back pocket of her jeans.

"She has it," Conor reported.

"Tell *her* to call Teresa then," Sean instructed. "It's better for us to stay out of this."

Apparently Charlotte had overheard Sean because she was already swiping open her phone when Conor started to tell her what to do. She rose, the phone pressed between her ear and shoulder, and let the blanket fall to the chair. "Terri? I need your help . . ." Her voice faded as she walked into the kitchen.

A surge of pride welled up in him as he watched her take a deep breath and straighten her shoulders. That was his Charlotte, always ready to face her dragons. And like so many times before, the dragons were her own kids. He couldn't imagine the pain of that. "Okay, she's calling Teresa," he said to Sean.

"Good. Hopefully, she'll be out of there before Rob turns up, and he's bound to. So what are you going to do when he does?"

He could practically hear Sean strategizing in his head.

Conor settled deeper into the buttery leather sofa, wishing like crazy that Sam was still there. She'd been gone five minutes and he already ached for her. He rubbed his hand over his face and tried to focus. "I'll just tell him she's not here. Even if she still is, I'll tell him she's not."

"Good idea." Sean heaved a huge sigh. "I have to say I'm not a bit surprised those two pushed her to this point."

"I guess that proves our theory that they were behind this whole mess from the get-go." Conor put his feet on the tool chest/coffee table and crossed his ankles.

"Yup. Harry will take it from here. He'll file a motion for

dismissal, a judge will have to sign off, and then the court will decide whether she'll be able to file the suit again at a later date. Hopefully, they'll tell her she can't."

Conor furrowed his brow. "Why would she do that?"

"Why did she contest in the first place, little brother?" Sean's tone was wry. "Who knows what her kids will try next."

"Will we be fighting this battle for the rest of her natural life?" Conor's stomach knotted. He sure didn't want *that* possibility hanging over his relationship with Char—he and Ali needed her to be Grammy and Mom, not an adversary.

"Nah." Sean chuckled. "I'd be surprised if Char didn't tell them both to beat it. I know it's probably wrong as heck that she prefers her steps to her own kids, but they've done this to themselves by constantly trying to manipulate her. Sounds to me like she might be over it."

"I *am* over it." Charlotte tucked her phone back into her hip pocket as she strode into the living room. "I can hear him, but put him on speaker anyway, Conor."

Conor did as he was instructed, amazed at the change in his stepmother. She'd smoothed her hair and tucked in her shirt.

A trace of a smile crossed her lips as she plopped down on the sofa and elbowed Conor gently while she spoke to both brothers. "I owe all four of you an apology. I'm so sorry I let this happen. The lawsuit was a terrible mistake." When tears appeared on her lashes, she swiped them away with her palms. "I'm asking you to forgive me. . .please."

Sean spoke up first. "Oh, Char, of course we forgive you. You got sidetracked. It's okay. It's over now, right?" Doubt edged his tone ever so slightly, but it was evident even across the miles.

Charlotte gulped and nodded decisively. "It's over. I'll have Harry help me drop the suit, and I'm sending Rob back to Louisville. I need a little space between me and those two for a while. I only hope I haven't destroyed my relationship with you four boys. You are more family to me than Rob and Sabrina ever thought of being." She gazed down at her canvas shoes and blinked, before raising her head and looking Conor straight in the eye. "I'll understand if you want me to go."

"Char, no." Conor reached out and tugged her gently into the circle of his arm, where she rested her head on his shoulder. "Lady, you've been our mother for the last twelve years. I, for one, can't imagine this family or this winery without you."

"I second that!" Sean's hearty agreement came through loud and clear. "I know Bren and Aidan will agree."

"Thank you." She put an arm across Conor's chest and squeezed him tight. "Thank you both so much." Pulling away, she sniffled, then wiped her nose on a tissue she'd grabbed from the half bath. "Terri should be here in a few minutes, so—"

"Mom!" A shout and a loud banging on the door interrupted her and she and Conor exchanged tight-lipped looks, the mood of which was echoed in Sean's "Don't answer that!" from the phone's speaker.

Conor handed her his phone, strode to the door, and peered through the peephole. "Well, it's not Teresa, unless she's grown a beard since yesterday and decided to start calling you *Mom*."

"Sean?" Charlotte rose too, clutching Conor's cell phone. "Why don't I just talk to him now?"

"He looks pretty pissed," Conor said over his shoulder.

"It would be better if you didn't." Sean's voice echoed from the phone in the large high-ceilinged space. "He'll have a stronger case against you if he can claim we influenced you."

"He's going to wake up Ali." Her brows furrowed and she brought the phone to Conor.

The concern for his daughter touched his heart. That was the Charlotte he knew and loved. "Char, go into the half bath, shut the door, and call Teresa. Tell her to pick you up at the winery. I'll keep Rob occupied while you grab a jacket off the pegs by the back door. You know where to find my cart keys." He tipped his chin at her. "They're in that basket by the door. Slip out through the screened porch as quietly as you can and take my cart up to meet her."

"Good plan, Bro," Sean said.

"Okay." Charlotte gave the door a dismissive glance and sighed before she squeezed his bicep quickly and headed through the kitchen.

"I'm leaving you on speaker, Sean." Conor set the phone on the bench by the door and turned the dead bolt, wondering if Sean might figure out a way to record the conversation. Was it even legal to record Rob without his permission? Hell, who knew and at this point, Conor didn't give a damn. He just hoped Sean was somehow saving the conversation for posterity; they'd worry about admissibility later.

Rob had managed to compose himself enough that when Conor opened the door, his stepbrother's expression no longer reflected anger, but rather concern. "Con, is Mom here?" He pushed past Conor and rushed in. "I can't find her. I'm afraid she's had some kind of breakdown or something."

"What happened?" *I can't wait to hear this story.*

Rob shivered and shrugged his shoulders, tucking his hands under his arms as if to warm them. "Damned if I know. She was out in the kitchen, cleaning up and I went into the living room to put on a movie. Seemed like it was taking her a long time to rinse off a couple of plates, so I popped in to check on her and she was gone. Left the water running in the sink. As far as I can tell, she just dropped everything and walked out."

"Did you check the garage for her car? Maybe she needed to run an errand." That was inane, but he was trying to give Char enough time to get out of the house. "Did she say anything about needing to go out?"

"No." Rob shook his head. "We were going to watch a movie. Her coat is still in the closet and her purse is on the desk where she always leaves it."

"What about her phone?" Conor tried to sound as worried as he should be, but he could imagine Sean grinning at his rather weak acting skills. This undoubtedly would become family lore, told and retold at holiday dinners.

"I didn't find it. I went through her purse and it wasn't there."

Ah, but I bet you found whatever cash she might have had in there, you slimy bastard.

Conor had to bite his cheek to keep from laughing and he was sure Sean had muted the mic on his phone. "Was her car in the garage?"

"Yes and so was the golf cart." Rob released a frustrated breath. "I'm worried sick about her, Conor. She's been acting weird lately anyway. Surely you've noticed how she's forgetting things. She'd totally spaced that I was coming up tonight. I think we're starting to see some dementia."

"Oh, come on, Rob. Dementia?" Conor scoffed. "She's only sixty-six years old and she's healthy as a horse."

"Her health has nothing to do with the state of her mind." Rob paced toward the kitchen, but as casually as possible, Conor cut him off and led him toward the living room. "Sabrina said she called her the other day and Mom didn't recognize her voice." He managed an Oscar-worthy stricken look. "Her own daughter! We've got to find her. She could be confused somewhere or . . . or hurt."

"Or maybe she just needed some fresh air. Did you check her patio out back? Maybe she walked up to the gazebo; she does that sometimes when she needs to think." Conor was grasping at straws, but he wanted to be sure Char was well on her way.

"I think I should call the police." Rob pulled his phone out and tapped the screen.

"Have you tried calling or texting her?" Conor eyed the window behind Rob, watching for the golf cart headlights.

Ah-ha, there they are.

Char was out the door and headed for the winery. The sodium vapor lights along the gravel drive revealed Teresa's little sedan creeping up toward the barn, headlights off. He rubbed his face to hide his smile while his stepbrother stared at his phone and texted Charlotte. No doubt Teresa was getting a kick out of the cloak-and-dagger of the situation. It would be the talk of the diner in the morning.

"Nothing from her and she's not answering my calls or my texts." Rob shoved his phone back in his pocket. "We need to figure out what to do with her, man."

"We?" Connor gaped at him.

What a nervy little jerk.

"Well, she's going to be part owner of this winery pretty soon, but if she doesn't have the mental capacity to function, we're all going to have to come up with a different plan." Rob's back was still to the window as he eyed Conor, who was having a very hard time keeping his temper in check.

"Look, Rob, I know what you're up to and it's not going to work." He moved into Rob's direct line of sight, trying to keep him from the windows that overlooked the winery. "You and I both know there's not a single thing wrong with Char's mind."

"What do you mean?" Rob lifted his chin and stared down his nose at Conor. "My concern is my mother—"

"Oh, please," Conor cut in and barked a grim laugh. "You don't give two sh—"

Suddenly Rob's phone dinged. When he checked the text he'd received, his entire demeanor changed. His face suffused with color, his brow furrowed, and his eyes darkened. "It's from Mom. She's with Teresa." He dropped the phone in his pocket and raised his head to face Conor, his face twisted in anger. "Listen, Conor, I don't know what that lady lawyer said to her the other night, but I do know that she didn't tell her who she was and why she's here. That's about as unethical as you can get."

This time Conor did laugh. "Are *you* seriously talking to *me* about ethics? That's rich."

"You two have been working on her. I know you have!" Rob's voice trembled with anger. "I knew it when she told me tonight that she wanted to drop the lawsuit."

"She said she wanted to drop the suit?" Conor said a little louder than necessary, mostly because he was hoping Sean was recording all this.

"Yes, dammit." Rob stomped his foot like a recalcitrant child. "She's been cantankerous as hell ever since we started this whole contest and—" He snapped his jaw shut, clearly aware that he was in imminent danger of overplaying his hand.

Conor crossed his arms over his chest. "You convinced her to do this, didn't you?" he asked calmly. "You and your sister."

Rob gazed at him for a moment, his expression changing from angry to supercilious. "So what if we did? She was getting screwed and she didn't even realize it."

Please, please, Sean, be recording this. Even if all we can do with it is intimidate him by letting him know we've got him on tape.

"Da left her in good shape and she knows she's welcome here as long as she chooses to stay." Conor kept his voice even. "We love Char and we'll take care of her until she draws her last breath."

Rob's eyes narrowed almost to slits, anger coming to the fore again. "You arrogant son of a bitch! For the last twelve years, you and your brothers have done everything you could to turn Mom against me and Sabrina. She barely knows we're alive because she's so in love with the Flahertys." Rob's voice rose almost an octave as his fury wound up. "Well, if she loves working at this damn winery so much, it's only right that she owns part of it. Donal told me last time I saw him that he planned to change his will to give her a fifth and—"

"That's crap!" Sean's voice thundered from the bench by the front door. "That's crap and you know it!"

Rob swung around and glared at the phone. "Has he been here the whole time?"

"Since before you pounded on my door," Conor replied, sauntering over to pick up his phone. "We all know Da never discussed his personal finances or the business of this winery with you."

"But . . . but he . . . he owes us . . . *her* . . ." Rob sputtered.

Conor reached for the doorknob. "I think it's time for you to go. And if you want to preserve even a shred of your relationship with your mother, you'd be wise to head back to Louisville, and both you and your sister lay low for a while. If you show up on my property uninvited again, I will call the sheriff."

"You can't keep me from my mom's place."

"Technically, I own that house, so I can. Right, Sean?" Conor held the phone up.

"Yep." His brother's voice was strong as Conor opened the door, letting in the cold night air.

"Get out, Rob," Conor said. "You can sleep at your mom's tonight since she's not there, but you'd better be gone in the morning."

Rob glowered at him for a long moment before turning on his heel and stalking out the door, his footsteps heavy on the wooden floor of the porch. Conor stood in the open doorway, watching while he got in his car, started the engine, and sped down the driveway, his tires spitting gravel.

Conor rolled his eyes. He was going to have to send Nate out there tomorrow after school to rake the rocks out of the grass. As he shut the door and turned the lock with a firm click, he heard Sean's chuckle over the speaker.

"Well played, little bro, well played."

Chapter Fifteen

AFTER A QUICK glance at the clock on the nightstand, Sam flipped her pillow over and burrowed deeper into her warm comfortable bed at the Serendipity. Six o'clock was too early to get up. Even though she had a list of things she needed to do today, it was still dark as midnight. A towboat's horn blasted mournfully as it pushed a tow of barges up the river—a sound she'd learned to love in just the few days she'd been in River's Edge. She wondered if it was loaded with coal or recycled iron or maybe timber. She'd googled *barges on the Ohio* last night when she couldn't get to sleep and found out they were one of the most inexpensive ways to move freight. Funny, she'd never been curious about the barges on the Chicago River or Lake Michigan, but everything about River's Edge fascinated her.

Her thoughts went to Four Irish Brothers, but this morning, she wasn't wondering what her next steps were in saving the winery. All she had left to do was meet with Harry to grab a copy of the dismissal paperwork that would close out the suit. No, this morning, her mind—and heart—were filled with a certain blue-eyed winemaker whose kisses left her breathless and longing for more. She rolled to her back, pushing the covers off her chest as her body flushed with heat and desire. What would've happened on that big leather couch last night if they hadn't been interrupted? Smoothing her hands over her belly, she groaned softly as she remembered Conor's seeking hands on her waist and his lips hot and hungry on hers. Dear God, how she wanted him . . . and not just because he knew how to kiss, although heaven help her, he was a world-class kisser. It was more than that.

She wanted to know everything about him. They'd barely scratched the surface last night, but the more he shared of his story, the more she hungered to learn. Questions filled her mind from the most mundane to the transcendent. What was his favorite color? Did he like his marshmallows toasted golden brown or burned black? Where did he see his life in five years? In thirty years? Despite the sorrow he'd experienced, he seemed so grounded. She envied him the camaraderie of this small community, his closeness to his family, and his genuine love of the vineyards and his calling as a winemaker.

Truth was she hadn't yearned like this for a man since college and Andy. And like Andy, Conor Flaherty was turning her sensible world inside out. Her heart had melted last night when he'd talked about his Emmy, when Sam had seen the home he was creating for his daughter. His love of the land and his devotion to his family's business were evident in the careful way he'd walked through the winery as he closed up, making certain everything was safe before he turned out the lights and locked the doors. His smile had shone with satisfaction when he gazed out over the hills before he'd bundled Ali into the car and led the way over the winding road through the vineyards to his house.

Conor was the guardian of his family's legacy, devoted to his brothers and to their father's dream, to his child and to this small river town. His life was here and there was certainly no room in it for a long-distance relationship. How could they possibly make that work? Who would look after Ali if he came up to Chicago? How did she even date someone when they had a small child to care for? Ali's sweet face popped into Sam's head and she smiled, recalling the little girl peppering her with questions as she'd tucked her in. The girl needed a mother and Sam had no idea how to be a parent.

Speculation was ridiculous of course because she'd only known him for a few days and besides, she didn't believe in love at first sight. That was not how grownups did it. Rushing into a relationship was always a mistake. Smart people took it slow, got to know one another, waited to see if their lives were a fit.

Her conscience nudged her. *Yeah, that sure worked well with you and David.*

She tucked her hands behind her head and sighed. Not a good example because she'd known from the very beginning she and David Walter Grant weren't a good fit. But it had been easy and it made her mother very happy—something Sam had rarely been able to do on her own. Oh, she and David had gotten along well enough and shared common interests—work, the theater, museums, decent films, and an evening at the symphony . . . but his touch didn't burn and she never ached for his kisses. After three years of predictable dates, just being with him had become a chore and she'd started to dread allowing his mechanical lovemaking. It wasn't the thought of a lifetime of by-the-book sex that ultimately made her grateful the relationship had ended though; it was the idea of a by-the-book life. And yet, wasn't she still living that life? Even without David in it?

She jumped when her phone beeped on the nightstand next to her. Who was texting her at six thirty in the morning? She scooped it up and swiped the screen.

"Sean told me not to contact you until today—it's today now, right?"

She grinned. It was Conor and she imagined him lying in the big brass bed she'd seen when she'd peeked into his bedroom last night. Did he wear pajamas or was he bare-chested in just a pair of boxers? She pictured him lean and muscled, his hair dark against the pillows, and her belly flipped over while a bolt of desire flashed through her. She closed her eyes for a second before thumbing her screen.

"Barely. How's Char?"

"Just texted with her. She's fine. Harry's getting the dismissal arranged this morning. He'll contact you with the paperwork."

"Sounds good. Is Rob still around?"

"No idea. I told him to clear out."

"For Char's sake, I hope he listened."

"Want to meet me at Mac's at 8? Please say yes."

Sam couldn't help grinning. Did she want to meet him? Dear Lord, yes! Resisting the urge to invite him to join her in her warm bed at Serendipity, she simply typed . . . *"Yes."*

And waited for the smiley face or clapping hands or thumbs-up that any other guy would've sent. Her heart pounded when what he sent back was . . .

"See you then."

All spelled out with a period at the end. No *CU* or waving hand. He was completely unaware, of course, that he was winning her over with this one stupid thing—this texting stuff, and maybe Sam set too big a store by how a guy communicated, but an economy of words correctly spelled and punctuated warmed her heart. Although, if she were truly honest with herself, she'd have to admit Conor Flaherty had warmed her heart simply by tossing her his incredibly sexy smile. She pressed the phone to her chest, feeling a lot like the twenty-year-old college student who'd received a love song in an email so many years ago.

The scent of fresh-brewed coffee drifted up to her room. Rose was up and making breakfast for her guests. Sam threw off the covers, shivered in the morning chill, and flipped the switch on the gas fireplace. A puff of air and then flames flickered around the logs. She stood in front of it, warming herself and gazing in the mirror above the mantel.

Last night, she'd packed her clothes and laptop, prepared

to leave for Chicago after she'd met with Harry and dropped Donal's journals off at the winery. But maybe she didn't have to leave immediately. She still had to go to Big O up on the highway and get her tire replaced, and hadn't she promised Ali that she'd be there for the tree lighting on the square? Of course, that was before Charlotte had dropped the suit and ended Sam's reason to stay. But she could at least stay for a little while and see Ali sing. She hated the thought of disappointing the little girl who'd stolen her heart.

Sean had encouraged her to stay for a few days when they had spoken last night and had repeated the instruction in the text he'd sent her later letting her know Char was safely at Teresa's, that she was definitely dropping the suit, and that Conor had handled Rob. A fiendish little smile appeared on her face in the mirror as she thought about outsmarting Charlotte's ungrateful children. She hoped that jerk was on his way back to Louisville with his tail tucked between his legs. Charlotte deserved better and she had it in the Flaherty boys; that was obvious from the concern Sam saw in Conor's face when his stepmother appeared on his porch. And even though it meant her job here was done, she was glad Charlotte had dropped the lawsuit against Four Irish Brothers. The winery belonged to Donal's sons and would no doubt be passed down to the generations that followed.

And there would be generations to come—Conor would marry again and some lucky lady would help him raise Ali and probably give him more children. Sons with their father's blue eyes and toffee-streaked brown hair . . . Would it be Megan, the mayor, or Tierney, with whom he clearly shared a special bond? Or, perhaps one day, a beautiful stranger would waltz into the winery and knock his socks off. She pressed her fist against her mouth to keep from gasping aloud at the thought of some other woman in Conor's arms. Why did that make her heart ache so? They barely knew each other and that wasn't going to change even if she stayed for a couple more days. Their lives were too different . . . simply too different.

"Stop it, you idiot!" She scolded her wild-haired, huge-eyed reflection. "Just stop it. Go have breakfast with him, enjoy a couple more days here, but keep it casual and light. You can do that. You're the master of casual and light, aren't you? It's not a commitment." With a last long look in the mirror, she shook her head. "It's not." She turned on her heel, and headed for the shower.

CONOR'S PHONE RANG just as he slid back into his SUV after dropping Ali at preschool. It was Brendan, who rarely called this early in the morning. He must've talked to Sean about Charlotte and was phoning to rehash the whole situation, which was a Flaherty thing. The four brothers had processed out loud to each other from the time they could all talk.

"Hang on, Bren." He started the car, flipped on the heater, and waited for the call to Bluetooth to the car radio. "You still there?"

"Dude!" Bren's deep voice was unusually animated. Conor was closest to his second oldest brother, probably because they were the two middle children. Sean, as oldest, always seemed to be in charge and Aidan, who was the baby and a big ham to boot, never failed to grab most of the attention when the four of them were together.

Brendan was an analyst for the CIA—a job he rarely ever discussed, smiling Sphinx-like whenever anyone asked him about his work. Aidan mercilessly teased him about being a *Jack Ryan,* Tom Clancy's adventuresome character in several novels, something Bren neither confirmed nor denied. Even though he lived in Germantown, Maryland, just outside of Washington, DC, he and Conor didn't let the six hundred miles between them affect their closeness. They talked or Skyped at least twice a week, sometimes more, particularly since Bren had been worrying about Conor and his grief over losing Emmy.

This morning though Brendan surprised him. "Hey, Conny, I've got Sean and Aidan patched in, too. Everybody here?"

"Yup," Sean answered, while Aidan's quick, "You betcha," was a bit fuzzier. Good God, it was five in the morning in LA.

Conor chuckled. "Aidan, what are you doing up at this hour?"

"I've got an early call this morning, but mostly I wanted to be in on the celebration." Aidan's voice brightened. "So tell us what's going on. Sean said Char appeared on your doorstep last night?"

"She did." Conor proceeded to regale his brothers with the whole story as he drove the few miles to Mac's and parked in one of the few remaining diagonal spaces outside the diner. He noticed Sam's car in the parking lot at Rose's. Maybe she was walking to the diner. He scanned the sidewalk on either side of Mac's, but didn't see her.

"So it was those brats of hers all along." Bren didn't even try to hide the contempt in his voice.

"We knew it!" Aidan piped in. "Man, I hope she's finally figured out those two are just big users."

"It's got to be hard to realize your own kids are so sleazy," Sean mused and took a deep sip of what would be coffee, black with one sugar. "We're all going to have to stand by her. She's going to need our support."

"Of course. She knows she can depend on us for anything," Brendan said around a mouthful of something—probably granola because that was his breakfast of choice. Bren didn't eat red meat, but he ate eggs and dairy and fish and poultry. The rest of the brothers were carnivores of the first order, but Brendan had given up meat in college.

"Harry is drawing up the paperwork to dismiss the suit

and he'll file it for her, so all she has to do is sign and we are done," Sean declared. Conor smiled as his brothers' cheers filled his car.

"So, Conny . . ." Bren began and Conor held his breath. When Bren started a sentence with *"So"* . . . something personal was coming. "Tell us about this Sam Hayes."

"Yeah, Sean says she's hot," Aidan chimed in and Sean instantly denied ever having said such a thing. But Aidan continued right over him as if he'd never spoken. "I think I may have met her when we were in Chicago last time. Tall, lots of shiny reddish-brown hair, great eyes, kinda serious?"

Conor debated for a moment. If it were just Bren on the phone, he would open up immediately about how attracted he was to Sam, and the two of them would hash out all the new feelings he'd been having the past few days. But he wasn't ready for Sam to be a topic of brotherly speculation. He had to sort out his own emotions first, see if this was something that was going to go anywhere. "You know, she's a . . . a nice person." *A nice person? Seriously? She's gorgeous and intelligent and sensitive and* . . . He stopped his train of thought when he realized he'd gone silent on his brothers. Clearing his throat, he added, "And she has a great palate. She loved Da's 2010 chambourcin."

"A great *palate*?" Conor could just imagine Aidan's blond eyebrows shooting up. "That's a new way of putting it."

"You gave her the *chambourcin*?" Brendan and Sean asked the question almost in unison and Conor couldn't help cracking up. They all knew the significance of offering someone Da's chambourcin.

"Yes. It's our best wine and I knew she'd appreciate it and she did. That's all." Just then, Conor caught sight of Sam, striding up from the River Walk; her cheeks were rosy from the chilly air while tendrils of hair that had escaped her severe bun curled around her ears and down her neck. His gut tightened as she drew nearer, and he forced himself to sit tight and not jump out of the car and race across the street to greet her. "I gotta sign off, bros, I've got a . . . a meeting at eight."

"He's got a *meeting*." Aidan's voice was full of innuendo. "I believe our dear brother may be coming out of the darkness, guys, and I think we might have Sam Hayes, attorney at law, to thank for it. So what's the deal? Talk to us."

"There's nothing to talk about," Conor replied absently as he watched Sam cross the street to the diner, smiling as she stopped to admire Clyde's antique Christmas tree.

"Leave him alone, Aidan." Sean's voice took on the big-brother tone he'd used all their lives to put them in their places. "If something's brewing, it's his affair."

"Exactly!" Aidan chortled. "I want details."

"I'm curious, too," Brendan admitted, "because you sound more animated than I've heard you in two years. And I'm fairly sure it's not just the fact that Char's dropping the suit or the pleasure of parenting our darling niece that's put a grin in your voice."

"I'm relieved beyond words that Char's changed her mind and Ali is always my greatest joy, but as for the rest, I'm pleading the fifth for now," Conor hedged. "Gotta go. Love you, bros." He tapped the screen before any one of the three of them could reply and pulled his keys out of the ignition.

Sam was only a block away. All he had to do was zip into the diner to snag a booth in the back so they could talk without distractions or interruptions. And after that, well, who knew what would happen?

Chapter Sixteen

"COME ON, SAM! Hurry up, Da!" Ali skipped ahead, the pompom on her pink hat bobbling as she ran along the River Walk. White lights, strung from tree to tree, lit the way for Sam and Conor, who followed at a more leisurely pace behind the little girl. Sam's hand was warm in Conor's and the evening was clear and brisk, the air crisp and smelling faintly of the river. A barge covered in Christmas lights chugged by and the tugboat captain tooted his horn when Ali stopped to wave.

"What a perfect night for a tree lighting." Sam paused to watch the barge for a moment, amazed at the twinkling reflections in the river. It was breathtaking.

"We specialize in perfect nights here in River's Edge." Conor pressed a quick kiss on her temple, his breath warm against her skin. "You should see how beautiful this path is in springtime when the redbud trees are blooming. Washington, DC's got nothing on us with those hokey cherry blossoms." He winked and Sam rolled her eyes.

This had to be reason number seven hundred and twelve that Conor had devised for her to stay in River's Edge. He'd been working hard for the last two days to convince her to stay longer and explore the irrefutable attraction between them. Sam couldn't deny he was tempting her almost beyond her ability to resist. For two days, he'd wined and dined her and then wined her again.

They'd tramped through the vineyard as he explained the intricacies of growing grapes in the hills of southern Indiana. She'd sat enthralled as he shared the history of the Ohio River Valley AVA appellation and how the area was actually the birthplace of American viticulture. Sam couldn't help the connection she felt watching Ali dance like a tiny fairy up and down the dormant vines while Conor pointed out the different varieties of grapes he grew. Her heart clutched, knowing she'd never see that sweet child grow into the beautiful woman she was destined to be.

Evenings, they cooked together in Conor's gourmet kitchen—on Thursday, she'd made butternut squash bisque after calling Aunt Bette for the recipe. A trip to the grocery up on the hill provided all the ingredients, and Sam had never enjoyed grocery shopping as much as she did with the Flahertys. Ali gamboled ahead of them, adding cookies and cereal and ice cream to the cart. Of course, Conor took the items right out again, although when both she and Ali pouted, he put the peppermint Oreos back in.

Already familiar with Ali's bedtime ritual, she relished the few minutes she shared with the little girl reading a story and singing. The first night, Sam had to confess she wasn't sure she knew any songs by heart, but the little girl had insisted, naming several tunes that Sam didn't recognize. Finally, from the depths of her own childhood memories, she'd managed to pull out a song that Aunt Bette used to sing to her. An old James Taylor melody, "You've Got a Friend." She'd messed up the words several times; however she managed to get through at least one verse and the chorus. Ali didn't seem to mind her rusty contralto, closing her eyes and hugging her stuffed rabbit as Sam slipped off the canopied bed.

After Ali was tucked in and sleeping, there was time for her and Conor to talk and touch and kiss by the fire. Just the thought of his eyes hungry with need, his fingers sifting through her hair, and his lips softly exploring her throat and ear sent a shiver through her. Somehow she'd managed not to give in to the desire raging through her, and even though Conor had not pushed, she recognized his ache matched hers. There was magic between them—something Sam hadn't known in so long it frightened her. For a week, she'd been a part of something she'd never experienced before—a real family—and the sensation of belonging to something bigger than she'd ever known overwhelmed her.

"Sam, see the boat lights!" Ali pointed to the barge and tugboat and waved furiously.

"That's far enough, Alannah," Conor called as Ali stepped closer to the edge of the gravel River Walk. "Stay on the path. Be careful."

"I am." Ali balanced precariously on the wood timber that lined the walkway. "Only my toes are over. See?" She teetered and Sam, acting out of pure instinct, jogged up to grab the child and swing her back into the middle of the path.

"You're giving me heart failure, kiddo." She tweaked Ali's cheek. "If you fell, you'd be in the river before we could say *'Ali, be careful.'*"

"Da already said that." Ali's grin sent a spasm of longing through Sam, and the tender expression on Conor's face as their eyes met over the little girl's head told her he knew exactly what she was feeling.

"Well, you should listen to him and stick to the path." Her voice was rougher than she intended, so she softened the words by smiling and extending a hand that Ali grasped. Conor took his daughter's other hand and the three of them walked the rest of the way to the town square.

"THERE SHE IS!" Char grasped Sam's bicep as she pointed with the other hand. "Oh, how darling are those little Santa hats?"

Sam grinned down at her, just as taken in as Ali's grandmother by the sight of the little ones coming onstage. "Are those knitted? Who did that?"

"They're knitted *and* crocheted." Char nodded, her smile

widening. "My homemakers club made them. We make them for preemies at the hospital, and Karen Cole, the preschool teacher, asked us to make some bigger ones for her class. That's Karen in the red dress. She's just great with these kids." She clasped her hands in front of her chest. "They turned out so darn cute, didn't they?"

"They're adorable," Sam agreed and saw her breath as she spoke. She shrugged her camel-hair coat closer, grateful for her knitted scarf and gloves and for Conor's big warm body next to her.

His fingers wrapped around hers and he pulled her closer to him when Ali's preschool class lined up on the stage the town maintenance crew had erected near the steps of city hall on the square. The little ones were the first ones up on the program and magically, all fifteen of them seemed to be paying attention to Karen and her assistants. They made a circle around the tree and sang a charming little song about a twinkling Christmas star and then did the reindeer *hokey pokey,* which had the audience that filled the square in stitches. They sang a little ditty about snowflakes complete with hand gestures that nearly each of them got right, although Ali did spot her da and stopped to wave, much to the delight of the crowd. Sam felt so at home among the laughing parents and grandparents; the rightness of it all made her eyes misty.

Then Ali came out of the line and Karen handed her a wireless mic. Sam glanced up at Conor. "What's she going to do?" The little girl hadn't mentioned having a solo any of the numerous times she'd practiced her songs for Conor and Sam.

He looked equally mystified. "I don't know. She never told me she had a solo or anything special." He tugged Sam closer to the front, while she reached for Char's hand to bring her along. The crowd parted like the Red Sea for the three of them as Ali began to sing a sweet song about being a little Christmas bell that ended with the rest of the children joining her on the chorus of *ding-dong, ding-dong.*

Her sweet voice, clear and pure as new snow, brought a lump to Sam's throat and when she eyed Conor, his blue eyes shone with pride and unshed tears. She started to lay her head against his shoulder for a moment and bask in the moment when a voice behind them stopped her cold.

"It's times like this that I think how awful it is that darling Emmy is gone." Someone behind her stage-whispered, "Poor Conor. He must be heartbroken that she's not here to see this precious child grow up."

"Shh." Another voice hushed her. "He's right there."

"Where?"

"Up in front with that woman attorney from Chicago." The whisper got softer, but Sam could still hear bits and pieces of the conversation. "I saw them earlier holding hands on the River Walk."

"Really? I saw them, too, at Mac's yesterday and . . ." The first voice dwindled as the pair must have moved away, but Sam had heard enough to cause a stabbing pain in her chest.

Suddenly her cheeks were scorching hot. If she had heard that gossipy exchange, then surely others around them had heard it too. Conor had released her hand a moment before and moved closer to the stage to take pictures, so chances were good, he hadn't heard, but Char put a bracing arm around Sam's waist.

"Ignore it—small-town nosiness, sweetie," she whispered in Sam's ear.

But it wasn't the humiliation of being the subject of idle talk; that was to be expected in a small town. No, it was the comment about Emmy that crushed Sam. The whole town was aware of what she already knew—she would never be Emmy.

Chapter Seventeen

"**H**EY, GORGEOUS! BEAUTIFUL morning, eh?"

Sam smiled when Mac hollered as she stepped into the warm diner so redolent with the wonderful smells of bacon and coffee and cinnamon. The place was more than half full, and nearly every patron turned to smile at her and call out a friendly greeting. This would never happen at the Dearborn Avenue coffee shop in Chicago, where she stopped most mornings. The customers there barely glanced up from their phones long enough to order their usual lattes and designer coffees. They wouldn't think of saying anything to each other, unless they accidentally bumped someone. Then they might grunt an *excuse me* and move on.

She scanned the room and found Conor back in the corner booth, chatting with the pretty server who wore a red apron over jeans and a black MAC'S RIVERSIDE DINER T-shirt. A wave of desire nearly overwhelmed her when he caught her eye, tossed her his bone-melting smile, and crooked a finger at her in invitation. It took everything she had not to rush over and throw herself into his arms. Instead, she returned the smile, walked sedately to the booth, and acknowledged the server, whose name was Norma. Her pixie cut and outgoing manner reminded Sam of her friend Suz. God, she was going to miss this town, these people . . . all of it.

"Honey, Conor asked for two coffees, so I'm going to go grab those real quick and I'll come back for your order, 'kay?" Norma's smile displayed dazzling white teeth. "You just peruse that menu, although I'll tell you the Belgian waffle is the special today. Served with eggs any style, your choice of bacon or sausage, and real whipped cream. None of that spray stuff here at the Riverside."

Sam's stomach growled in response. "I'll take the waffle with bacon and may I have my eggs poached?"

"Oh, sweetie, you can have your eggs any way you want them." Norma accepted her menu and then paused to look expectantly at Conor. "You need a minute, big guy?"

"Nope." He shook his head and that errant curl fell over his forehead. "I'll have the waffle too, with sausage and scrambled eggs. Mac knows how I like 'em."

"So do I, handsome, so do I." Norma gave him a broad wink and sauntered off, hips swaying.

Conor shoved the lock of hair in place—pointless since it fell right back down again—and set his elbows on the red Formica table between them, resting his chin in his palm. "Hello." His voice was low and sexy, reminding her of the precious moments they had the previous night after Ali had gone to bed. The memory of his warm breath in her ear and on her cheek, his lips on hers, gentle at first and then his mouth taking hungry possession of hers made her heart speed up.

"G-good morning." Sam was sure he could hear her heart pounding. This was insane. All the effort she'd put in to becoming a sensible, in-control, cool career woman went right out the window in Conor Flaherty's presence. Suddenly she was tongue-tied and blushing like a high school freshman at her first dance. She closed her eyes for a second, then started over. "Where's Ali this morning?" At least her voice sounded calm, even if butterflies were doing acrobatics in her stomach.

"She's with Char—they're going Christmas shopping."

"How fun, she should love that." Sam leaned back as Norma set steaming mugs of coffee in front of them along with a miniature pitcher of half-and-half. "Thank you, Norma."

Conor smiled his thanks and got a pat on the shoulder in return from the server before she scooted off to take another order. "She's jacked—they're going to Target, which is Ali's all-time favorite store right now."

"Who doesn't love Target?" Taking a breath, she changed the subject. "You've been really generous with Char, given the trouble she's put you through." Sam sipped her coffee. "Although, I'm gonna bet she won't be so easily manipulated again."

Conor rolled his eyes. "Lord, I hope not. We do love her.

Being afraid we'd lose her was nearly as bad as the thought of having her kids in our business." After a moment of quiet as they both enjoyed their coffees, he finally asked, "What's your day like?"

Sam took a breath. "I'm going up to Big O to buy a new tire. After that, I'll probably check out of the Serendipity and be on my way back home. If I leave before lunch, I won't hit too much of the Saturday holiday shopping traffic."

A muscle worked in his jaw as he stared into his mug. When he looked up, his face was full of anticipation. "Wouldn't you rather come to the winery and help me put labels on the last fifty cases of Jingle Red?"

"What's Jingle Red? Wait"—Sam peered at him—"you do that by hand?"

Conor threw back his head and laughed—a deep joyful sound that sent a spasm of longing mixed with regret through her because it didn't really matter what Jingle Red was or how he put the labels on his wine bottles. She wasn't going to be there to help.

He eyed her for a moment. "Jingle Red is our Christmas wine—a blend of Leon Millot and Chancellor with a little foch. It's good for mulling. We have a machine that puts the labels on, but we do have to feed the bottles through. However, I can think of plenty of ways we can entertain ourselves in between cases." A dimple creased one cheek as he offered her a coaxing smile.

Sam met his eyes for the briefest of seconds before dropping her gaze to the swirly pattern of the tabletop. "Conor, I—" Breakfast arrived and she snapped her mouth shut as Norma placed fragrant waffles on the table along with their sides, then added a pitcher of warm maple syrup, and a bowl of fresh whipped cream between them. The food looked and smelled heavenly, but Sam's appetite had left her.

"Here we go, kids." Norma laid extra napkins on the table and gave them both a bright smile. "Can I get you anything else? Milk? Juice?"

"We're good, Norma, thanks." Conor picked up his fork and Sam followed suit.

"I'll be back around to warm up that coffee." She sashayed off to another table as Sam set her fork on her plate.

"I have to go home now." Sam's mouth had become so dry that the words came out in a near-croak.

"Why?" Conor poured syrup over his waffle and added a dollop of whipped cream. "Stay a while longer. If you leave now, you'll miss the candlelight walk. The luminarias are great fun—you don't want to miss those." He was trying to keep things light, she could tell, but his mouth pulled to one side and his eyebrows pinched together in a look of apprehension.

"Work is waiting for me. I have a meeting on Monday that I need to prepare for and I have a deposition to take and other cases that need my attention and . . ." She gazed at him hoping the longing she felt wasn't showing in her expression. The excuses were weak, but she had to go. She didn't really want to have this conversation in front of a diner full of townsfolk, but if she didn't leave now, it would be even harder later. "Please tell Ali good-bye for me."

"Sam, please. Don't go." Conor dropped his fork on his waffle without taking a bite. His voice was husky with intensity. "Stay. I'm so attracted to you and I-I know you're feeling the same way. You can't deny it."

"I'm not denying it, but, Conor, we hardly know one another." An endless tumble of raw thoughts and emotions spilled through her. She was lying to herself and to him. Yes, they'd only just met, but she'd known him all her life. He was the man she'd imagined herself falling in love with since she was a teenager. Except *that* fantasy man didn't already love someone else. He didn't have a child or a world that Sam would never fit into. She couldn't be what he needed and she couldn't stand to be there when he realized it. The look on his face made her heart hurt. How much worse would it be the longer she stayed?

CONOR SHOVED THEIR untouched plates aside and reached for her hand, lacing his fingers with hers. He wasn't about to let her just walk away. "What we have is good—I know it. I know because I've had it before. Some people search their whole lives for this and never find it. Yes, it's fast, but that doesn't mean it's not right."

A flurry of expressions chased across Sam's face settling in a tight, thin smile. "That's exactly why I have to go. You've had it before. What if I can't live up to what you had with Emmy? And this isn't about just you and me. There's Ali." She pulled away, hunching her shoulders and clamping her hands between her thighs. "I don't know how to be a mother. I wouldn't even know where to begin."

"I saw you with Ali; she adores you already." His stomach churned as he desperately racked his brain to find the words that would make her change her mind. "Let's focus on you and me right now. Just us."

Her head was bowed and when she lifted it, tears shimmered in her dark eyes. "There is no *us,* Conor."

"Maybe not yet. But there's the possibility of us." He leaned across the table and touched her cheek. "I know you feel it. I can see it in your face. These last couple of nights, it's been practically impossible for both of us to resist—"

She pulled her face away from his caressing fingers and swiped at her eyes. The sadness there was replaced with a look of cool determination. "Thank God we did. If we'd"— she blushed to the roots of her hair and ducked her head before looking him in the eye again—"well, it would've been a terrible mistake." Straightening her shoulders, she reached into her capacious tote and placed a brown paper sack on the table before gathering up her coat. "Here are your Dad's journals. Thanks for sharing them with me. He must've been a remarkable man. I wish I could've known him."

"Sam . . ." Conor's throat closed up. "Please . . . wait . . ."

She bit her lower lip as she rose from the booth. "I can't save you from your grief, Conor. I'm sorry."

Unprepared for such a full frontal assault, Conor jerked his hand back. He rubbed his fingers and palm across his mouth, massaging his jawline. A deep breath later, he caught her arm as she started to walk away. "*I* don't need to be saved from anything. You know what, though? I kind of think you do." He slid his hand down to grasp her fingers and then he softened his tone. "Don't throw this away, Samantha Hayes."

She closed her eyes and squeezed his hand before she released it. "Good-bye, Conor. Take care." Blinking back tears, she fled, shrugging into her coat as she hip-checked the heavy glass door and ran outside.

Chapter Eighteen

SAM HAD EXPECTED their good-bye to be difficult, however she'd underestimated how bereft she would feel. Her shoulders shook and hot tears stung her eyes as she practically ran down to the riverfront and up the path to the Serendipity. She hurried up the stairs with just the barest acknowledgement of Rose's sunny *good morning* from the dining room. Facing anyone at that moment was impossible. She couldn't bear kindness right now; one kind word and she'd break down for sure.

Slipping into her room, she closed the door and leaned against it, her breasts heaving as if she'd just run uphill for a mile. She couldn't breathe. Pressing her fists to her chest, she tried to take in some air. Oh, crap, was she *hyperventilating*?

Gathering strength, she pushed off the door, staggered to the dresser, and grabbed a paper bag from the little textile shop in town. Shaking out the colorful woven dresser scarf she'd bought for Aunt Bette, she crumpled the bag and breathed into it. It smelled of sandalwood and fiber, and after a few deep breaths, she was functional again.

She opened her window and dropped into the armchair

beside it, taking in long relaxing lungsful of fresh cold air. Eyes closed, she laid her head back and focused on yoga inhalation—in for four, out for four, in for four, out for four. At last, she began to feel more normal—except for the tears spilling over her lashes.

Dammit. Dammit. Dammit.

In just six days, she'd become exactly what her mother had always accused her of being—a sentimental, silly sap. Weeping over a man she'd known for mere days! Tears she should've shed when her three-year relationship with David had ended. No, when that romance went south, she'd gone to the beach and skipped in the moonlight. She rubbed the back of her neck and stared out across the wide river, loath to get up and finish packing. Checkout was eleven, so she had plenty of time, but common sense told her to get out before she changed her mind and raced back to him.

Walking out of the diner, turning her back on the handsome winemaker had been one of the hardest things she'd ever done. Harder than the bar exam. Harder than dealing with her mother when David broke their engagement. Not as hard as losing her dad, but the sadness felt the same. Her lip quivered and she swiped her nose with the back of her hand. Glancing around for a tissue box, she pulled herself out of the chair, went to the nightstand, and blew her nose.

Time to leave. Time to put River's Edge, Four Irish Brothers, and Conor Flaherty and his daughter behind her. She had a life in Chicago—a pretty darn nice life. A great career, good friends, purpose . . . She knew who she was in the city. Her life was reasonable, sensible, careful. Ever since she'd arrived in this sleepy river town, she'd turned into someone she didn't know. A woman full of overwhelming desires, nostalgia, and longing. That wasn't real life.

Real life was a tire that needed to be replaced. Real life was stopping by Harry Evans's office for the paperwork that ended the lawsuit against her client. Real life was getting on the road to Chicago so she could beat the traffic on the Skyway Bridge. Even better, she'd skip the trip to Harry's office. There was nothing she needed to sign. He could just mail her the paperwork. Quickly, she texted the white-haired attorney, asking if he could send the papers to her office in Chicago. Immediately he sent back a reply in the affirmative that made her lips curve up in a small smile. The message included a sad face emoticon, a broken heart, and a hand waving good-bye. Of course Harry would love emojis; that fit.

Shaking her head, she marched to the bathroom, washed her face, and repaired her makeup before gathering up her toiletries and tucking them into her suitcase among her folded clothes. Each item carefully placed, neat and tidy— just like her life.

"YOU GONNA LET her just walk out like that?" Tierney

Ashton, Emmy's best friend, slid into the seat across from Conor. A seat that was probably still warm from Sam's perfect behind.

"You heard that?" Conor picked up his fork, but it was sticky with syrup, so he dropped it on the table and reached for the one that Sam had abandoned only minutes before. The first bite of the waffle tasted like ashes, so he set that plate aside and focused on the sausage.

"We all heard it. You picked a heckuva place to declare yourself, bud." Tee leaned across the table and tapped his temple with one finger. "Go after her, idiot!"

Conor chewed the bite of sausage slowly and then took a sip of coffee, which had grown cold. He scowled and looked around for Norma. She was behind the counter, so he caught her eye and pointed to his mug. He met Tierney's gaze and shook his head. "No."

"Hey, handsome, you switched women on me here." Norma winked at Tierney as she poured steaming coffee into his mug. "Can I get you something, Tierney?"

"A stick so I can beat some sense into this guy?" She huffed and threw herself against the red vinyl-cushioned back of the booth.

Norma glanced from one of them to the other, then rolled her eyes heavenward. "Do you want your cup from the counter?" she asked Tierney.

"No thanks. I'm on duty in fifteen."

Tierney's eyes stayed on him as he took another bite of

sausage. She was waiting for him to say something; that much was clear. However, he was damned if he knew what to say, so he just kept eating.

"Conor, she's the best thing that's ever happened to you." Tierney waved her hands. "Strike that. She's *one* of the best things that's ever happened to you. But she's definitely the best thing lately."

"I know."

"Then what are you waiting for?" she asked, exasperation lacing her tone. "Why don't you go get her?"

"Because she clearly doesn't want to be gotten." He raised one brow at her and kept eating, even though his stomach was turning over.

All his instincts told him to bust out of the diner, chase Sam down, and beg her to stay. But there was a small voice in the back of his mind that reined in those desires. A voice he had learned to pay attention to in the last two years. He believed it was Emmy, guiding him from beyond and he'd never once regretted listening to it.

"Yes, she does!" Tee insisted. "It's written all over her face!" She turned around to the other diners, who were obviously listening. Hell, he would've been. And he had no doubt every single one of them had an opinion about him and Sam. "Don't you guys think so? Didn't you see it on her face?"

A murmur of agreement floated through the diner, and Mac came around from the kitchen with the question Conor was sure they were all thinking. "Why aren't you going after her, Con?"

"It's not time," Conor replied calmly and took up a forkful of cheesy scrambled eggs. "Not yet."

Tierney glared at him. "You're an idiot."

"Probably."

"She's loading her car!" Noah Barker announced as he peered out the front window from his table near the door. "I can see her in Rose and Tim's parking lot."

"What do you mean *not yet*?" Dot Higgins turned away from the cash register as Sheila rang up her carryout order. Dot came in nearly every morning for croissants and jam and coffee for her and her sister Mary to enjoy before they opened their quilt shop. "The romantic thing to do would be to go after her."

"You read too many lovey-dovey novels, Dot," Clyde Schwimmer declared as he rose from his place at the counter and peeled a couple of dollar bills from under the old-fashioned money clip he always carried in his pocket. "Women don't want to be chased anymore. They've got careers and their own lives to live. A guy's lucky if he can grab a gal on the run long enough for a drink and a goodnight kiss."

"That's a pretty cynical attitude, Clyde Schwimmer." Dot tossed him a saucy smile. "Especially coming from a man who's been married to the same woman for forty-five years and still brings his wife flowers every week." She winked. "Yeah, we see you coming out of Posy Pushers every Tuesday afternoon."

Conor couldn't help joining in the general amusement as Clyde's face turned bright red. "*She* chased *me*," he replied and then tossed a chin lift to Conor as he headed out the door. "You know what's right for you, Conor. Trust your manly instincts."

Laughter erupted again and Conor waved to Clyde. "Thanks, Clyde! I appreciate your support." Then he rolled his eyes as Noah offered up another report.

"She's driving away."

"Thanks for the update, Noah." Conor gave him a thumbs-up.

"So . . . not yet?" Tierney quietly repeated Dot's question when the rest of the diners had gone back to their own breakfasts, although he was pretty sure they all still had a small part of their attention focused on him. It was how River's Edge worked. "What does that even mean?"

"It means Sam needs time." Conor sipped his coffee and finished the last bite of scrambled eggs. As the knot in his stomach began to loosen, the waffle started to look good— delicious actually with maple syrup and melty whipped cream all over it. "I'm going to give it to her."

Tierney crossed her arms over her chest, her eyes narrowed as she watched him dig into the waffle. "Emmy would tell you to go after her."

Conor almost choked. He swallowed the bite of waffle

that threatened to stick in his throat before he very carefully set the fork down and wiped his lips with his napkin. "Tierney Ashton, you know I love you. We've known each other our whole lives. You're the little sister I never had, and I know you were Emmy's dearest friend, but do not"—he skewered her with a glare—"do *not* ever presume to tell *me* what Emmy would think."

"Oh, Con, I-I . . ." she floundered and color rose to her cheeks.

He immediately regretted his harsh tone. "I'm sorry, Tee." Reaching across the table, he grasped her hand. "Listen, honey. I'm not giving up. I know Emmy wanted—wants—me to be happy, to find love again. I think with Sam, maybe I can, but there's this . . . this voice in my head telling me to be chill and it sounds a lot like Emmy. So I'm going to be patient for a little while. I'll let it simmer, but when the time is right, I'll go for it, okay?"

Tierney squeezed his hand and her eyes glistened. "I can't tell you how good it is to have you back with us, Conor Flaherty. Even if that's all that comes from the Sam Hayes affair, which *is* what we've all been calling it, it's enough for me."

"I'll drink to that!" Noah stood up and lifted his coffee cup. "Norma, refills for everyone. We're celebrating. Conor's back at the Riverside, it's almost Christmas, and all's right with the world."

As everyone lifted their coffee cups and he raised his

hand in salute, warmth flooded Conor's soul and his heart lifted. It was a comforting feeling. Comforting in the way that something familiar and expected was always comforting. God, how he loved this town, these folks who were always in one another's business. The last week had given him more than just the possibility of love; it had given him back his life, his joy. Tierney was right, even if that was all that came of it, wasn't that something to celebrate?

He grinned at her. "The *Sam Hayes affair*? Seriously?"

She shrugged, yanked a napkin out of the holder to wipe her eyes, and put on her EMT jacket and hat. "What can I say? You're the talk of the town, dude." With a cocky wink and a little swagger, she left him to finish his waffle, and to ponder exactly how he was going to win the heart of a certain gorgeous, but stubborn, Chicago attorney.

Chapter Nineteen

"MORNING, MS. HAYES." Clark at the reception desk gave her his signature adorable smile—the one that had all the females at Stark, Randolph, Smith, and Flaherty swooning since he'd taken over the job two years earlier.

This morning however, Sam was immune to even Clark's undeniable charms. She nodded briskly. "Morning."

"Welcome back. We missed you." He tried harder and Sam had to give him credit; this time his dimples were even more pronounced than usual.

She smiled in spite of her foul mood. "Thanks, Clark. I appreciate you saying so."

She made her way to her office, stopping long enough to confer with her assistant, Margo, whom she shared with two other associates. She'd only been away a week, and her schedule had filled up with depositions, another settlement meeting with the Franklins—God help her—and two appointments with possible new clients.

First order of business was to check her email and then log the hours she spent on the Four Irish Brothers case, which she had to be honest didn't amount to much. Truth be told, she felt bad about billing any time at all; Sean would expect to receive an invoice though, so she spent a few minutes trying to figure out exactly what portion of her time in River's Edge was focused on the lawsuit.

That task finished, she moved on to her email and dealt with several that needed immediate attention. Although her thoughts were in such disarray, she frequently caught herself staring blindly at her screen while her mind was about three hundred miles due south. At one point, she simply closed her eyes and leaned back in her chair, unable to absorb anything she was reading because Conor Flaherty kept creeping into her brain.

Dear heaven, he was gorgeous, with his maple-syrup-colored hair hanging over his collar and falling across his brow when he was animated. The man needed a haircut, but there was something so sexy about his too-long mop and the smoky-blue depths of his gaze when he leaned down to kiss her. She shivered, remembering how her skin tingled when he stroked his thumb along her cheek or when he touched her hair, letting the curly strands tangle in his fingers. A frisson of passion went through her at the memory of his hands hot and insistent on her hip, then slipping under her sweater and heating her spine through the thin silk of her camisole.

She tried to imagine where he was right at that moment, which in River's Edge was an hour later than Chicago. He'd already have dropped Ali at preschool, maybe stopped by

Mac's for cheesy eggs and coffee before heading to the tasting room in town or back to the winery. Maybe he was putting the finishing touches on the Christmas tree in the high-ceilinged living room of his log house. She'd helped him drag his decorations out of the attic storage on Friday so he and Ali could trim the tree over the weekend. He'd believed she would still be there to help, but no doubt, Charlotte had joined them instead. She'd probably brought cookies and Ali would have had a couple with milk while Char and Conor shared a celebratory bottle of wine, cementing their closeness. Ali probably got into her cute footie PJs, Char might have braided her thick dark hair, and Conor would have let her tuck his daughter in because things were back to normal at the Flaherty's.

Nice picture of perfect familial bliss, Sam. However, it doesn't include you, so let it go.

Jerked back to reality with that notion, she straightened up and went back to answering emails. As she was sending off a note to a former colleague who had written to share the news of her new position in a big Washington, DC lobbying group, her computer dinged with another email. When she glanced down at the corner of her screen, she saw it was from Harold J Evans, esq. and a little paper clip icon indicated it had an attachment. Most likely a PDF of the dismissal paperwork.

She opened it and smiled as she read it. The note was pure Harry. No salutation or greeting, just picking up as if they were in the middle of a conversation.

Well, girlie, you ran away after a big win for our side. What's up with that? I sorta thought you'd stick around for a while. I wanted to talk to you about something I'm considering down here, hoped you'd give some thought to helping out an old country lawyer. Maybe I was wrong about what I saw brewing between you and Conor— maybe it was just wishful thinking on my part. I heard about you walking out on him at Mac's. Sure wish you'd stayed to see what developed though. He's a good man, and you two seemed like you had a spark between you.

Anyway, here's the signed dismissal—walked it to the courthouse myself and the judge approved it this morning—add it to the case file, but make sure Sean sees it. He gave me a big lecture last time he was in my office about how law firms need to move into the 21st century and be more ecologically sound. Dig me! This old hippie's going paperless!

Don't be a stranger, Sam, ok?

Harry

Her smile widened to a grin, even though she was blinking back tears. How could she miss the old gentleman so much when she barely knew him? In fact, how could she miss an entire town so much? She'd only spent a few days there. Somehow, though, she was certain Megan Mackenzie was a person she'd might have been friends with, and Tierney Ashton had such a sparkling personality that Sam had wanted to get to know her better, too. Her mind flew back to the folks at the tree-trimming party, all of them laughing and intimate and clearly close to Conor and Ali.

Alannah. Sam rolled her lips between her teeth and bit down. The child had scored a place in her heart when she'd begged her to return and whispered, *want to be best friends?* Sam recalled the sweet scent of Ali's soft hair as she cuddled with her on the pink comforter and read the Fancy Nancy book. Something frozen and long-buried inside her had thawed when Ali had asked her to sing a song after she'd finished the story.

Her heart ached remembering the little girl's long lashes against her pink cheeks—her dad's lashes—and the peaceful, even in-and-out of her breathing. Sam had tucked the comforter around her slight frame and tiptoed out even though she could've stayed and watched her for hours. What was it about the innocence and perfect purity of a sleeping child? Ali had been too young to know the real pain of her mother's death and she would never know the ugliness that Sam saw every day in her divorce and custody cases. But the child was obviously hungry for a mother's love, even though Conor was doing a great job as a single parent.

Sam had no idea how to be a mother, in spite of the yearnings that had begun upon meeting Alannah Flaherty. She wasn't cut out for motherhood and her damn biological clock needed to stop nudging her. She would screw it up and Ali needed someone who knew what it was to be a kind and caring mom. Sam's only experience had been her own cold fish of a mother who had sucked most of the joy out of her childhood years and continued, to this day, to look at her only daughter as though she were some kind of unusual bug. Her dad had filled in with fun when he was able, but often he was loathe to cross his wife and busy with a career that took him from the defense table to a judge's bench during Sam's growing-up years.

No, she wasn't parent material. It was nonsense to imagine she ever could be. What was the point in following her stupid, stupid heart and *giving it a try* as Conor put it? People who followed their heart very often ended up heartbroken. Sam could handle her own despair, but she simply could not fathom causing either Conor or Ali another moment of heartbreak when they discovered she could never be Emmy.

With a resolute sigh, she saved the PDF from Harry to the Four Irish Brothers file on her computer and sent a quick email to Sean that included that and the invoice. Time to close out that case and move on to the others that were waiting for her.

A few minutes later, Sean Flaherty appeared at her door. "Hey? What-what are you doing here?" His tie was askew and his toffee-colored hair, so like Conor's, was tousled as though he'd been raking his fingers through it.

She popped hear head up and gazed him over her computer screen. "Um, I work here?"

"I thought you were going to stay down in River's Edge for a while. Take a vacation." He leaned against the doorframe, his blue eyes alight. "You know, hang out and . . . and see the town all lit up for the holidays."

"The case was dropped. There was no need for me to stay."

"But . . . Conor said—" He stopped and shoved his hands into the pockets of his perfectly tailored suit pants.

"What?" Until now, she hadn't ever suspected that Sean had sent her down there for any reason other than to help Conor with the lawsuit. Suddenly, she wondered if he'd had an ulterior motive. Oh, no. Surely Sean Flaherty was *not* matchmaking.

"Never mind." Sean straightened to his full height and glanced at his watch. "Welcome back."

"Thank you." Sam watched as he backed away from her door, a frown furrowing his brow. When he got past Margo's desk, she saw him pull out his phone and break into a jog, his steps echoing on the marble floor of the hall.

CONOR SHUT DOWN the labeling machine when his cell vibrated against his thigh. Sean was calling. "Hey Bro. What's up?"

"Hey. How's it going down there?" Sean sounded a little breathless, like he'd been running. "I've got Bren patched in."

"Hey, little brother," Brendan spoke up. "You doing all right back there?"

Conor's curiosity was more than aroused. His brothers didn't usually call in the middle of the morning on a weekday, and if one of them did, it rarely turned into a conference call. "I'm fine. What's up with you guys?"

"Nothing," Sean said too quickly. "Do we always have to have a reason to call our kid brother?"

"Yeah." Bren jumped in. "Can't we just call to say hi?"

"Sure you can." Conor settled on the stool that stood next to the labeling machine. "I'm pretty sure that's not what you're doing, though. What's going on, guys?"

"Okay." Sean's breath was more even now. "We're just checking in with you."

"Why?"

"Sam's back in the office." Sean blurted it out and suddenly Conor knew exactly what was on their minds.

"I know. She left Saturday." He reached out to press an errant corner on one of the labeled bottles. The damn machine wasn't getting the whole label sealed again. He was going to have to take it apart and see what was going on. Maybe he just needed to trash the stupid thing and get a new one. This one had labeled a lot of bottles over the years.

"Yeah." Caution laced Brendan's voice. "And you're okay

with that, right?"

"No, but *I'm* okay, if that's what you're wondering." Warmth washed over Conor.

His brothers always had his back, even more since Emmy had died. He could imagine Sean's panicked call to Brendan when he saw that Sam was back in Chicago. They were all aware or at least they suspected that he and Sam had hit it off while she was here, and he was certain they were rooting for the relationship to take off. He knew how worried they'd been the past two years, although he hadn't been aware until now of just how low he must have seemed to them.

He truly hadn't understood it himself until suddenly he wasn't anymore, the moment when he realized he wanted Sam more than he wanted to join Emmy. And it wasn't just a physical attraction, although that was huge; he also wanted to know her mind and her heart, which she was clearly trying so very hard to protect. He wasn't sure yet how he was going to convince her she didn't need to protect herself from him, but he was working on it. Maybe it was time to talk to his brothers, get some ideas. Hell, it had been years since he'd, to use an old phrase of Da's, *wooed a woman.*

"That is what we're wondering," Bren confessed, chagrin overpowering concern in his tone.

"I thought she'd stay, man," Sean admitted. "And, okay, maybe subconsciously, I was matchmaking when I sent Sam instead of one of the other associates, but she needed a break and I've been thinking for a while that you and she might . . . you know, like each other.”

“Ah-ha!” Conor laughed. “Was she in on this?”

“No way, Bro!” Sean denied heatedly. “She'd break my balls if she knew I'd sent her down there with any ulterior motive. It just struck me that you two would get along.”

“We did.” Conor released a huge sigh and, man, did it feel good to open up and say the words. “We connected, you know? Just immediately. Even before I knew who she was. Did you know I changed her tire last Sunday? We didn't introduce ourselves or anything, but even then, there was something—I dunno.”

Sean chuckled. “That sounds intriguing.”

“It's like I've been released somehow and . . . don't laugh or think I've gone ’round the bend, as Da would say, but I keep feeling like Emmy is pushing me. The sadness is still there, I don't deny that. I'll always love Emmy, she's a part of me, but the possibility of something happening with Sam excites the heck out of me. Does that make sense?”

“Perfect sense, Conny.” Brendan's voice held a tinge of anticipation. “So, what are you going to do about it?”

“Yeah,” Sean added, “how come she's up here and you're down there?”

Conor shook his head before he realized his brothers couldn't see that, so instead he said, “I'm giving her a little time. She's running scared. I'll make my move soon. This feels too good for it not to be right.”

“Okay then,” Sean and Bren said in unison and they all

three cracked up.

"Don't wait too long, little brother," Sean advised.

"I don't think I'll have to," Conor replied, feeling way less confident than he sounded.

However, he did have a secret enticement in the form of a certain little four-year-old who he knew had stolen Sam's heart. He wasn't above playing that card if it brought Sam back to River's Edge, but he sincerely hoped he wouldn't have to. His little girl might've wanted a mother, but her father was also in want of a wife. And he had a sneaking suspicion that no one but Sam Hayes would do—for either of them.

Chapter Twenty

"DA, WHEN IS Sam coming home?" Ali slopped milk from her bowl of oatmeal on the table. "Whoops!"

Grabbing a paper towel, Conor wiped up the spill before she could get her sleeve in the mess because that would mean another ten minutes in front of her closet picking out a different shirt. God forbid anyone should have to go to preschool in a shirt that had been soiled with oatmeal and milk. Her other Christmas shirt was in the laundry, which reminded him he really needed to get some clothes washed.

He added a load of laundry to his mental checklist that also included restocking the tasting room in town with Jingle Red since Char had texted last night to let him know she was down to two cases, and figuring out why the dishwasher in the winery had suddenly stopped working. He needed to wrap the Princess Arendelle Castle Lego set and Elsa bike helmet that had arrived yesterday—thank God for online shopping—and the *Frozen* alarm clock that Ali had been begging for since she saw it at Target back before Halloween. His pre-Christmas to-do list was getting longer and longer and it was times like these that he really missed having a partner to share some of the load.

Emmy had loved everything about the holidays from baking pies and a turkey for Thanksgiving to shopping for gifts and putting up Christmas lights and garland. This was the first year that Ali was able to fully understand and participate in the Christmas celebrating, probably a good thing since this was also the first year since Emmy's death that Conor himself had felt like celebrating. Magic was in the air this Christmas, and he was convinced the feeling of enchantment had as much to do with Sam Hayes as it did with sharing the holidays with his little girl. He had no idea when or even if Sam would return, but simply the possibility of loving her had lifted the veil of grief. He was healing and that fact alone was enough to make this holiday season particularly joyful.

"Da?" Ali's sweet breath warmed his cheek as he wiped oatmeal off her face as well. "When is Sam coming home?" she asked more insistently.

Conor sighed. *Good question, kiddo.* "I dunno. This isn't Sam's home, Alannah. She lives in Chicago."

"I know, but she's going to move here and marry us," Ali declared and popped another blueberry into her mouth.

"What makes you so sure?" Conor sat down across from her with his coffee, a plate of cheesy eggs, and an English muffin slathered with peanut butter and jelly. Ever since Sam's arrival in his life, he'd been eating like a lumberjack. He hadn't been on a scale, but clothes that had hung loosely on him for almost two years were starting to fit like they should.

"I had a dream that she was here. She came with Santa Claus."

"Santa brought her? Like a gift?" He thought that sounded like the perfect Christmas present.

"Nooo." Ali tossed him a glance full of four-year-old disdain. "She came on his sleigh. He stopped in Chicago to pick her up and then brought her here."

"That was nice of him." Conor smiled at the picture in his head of his Sam, snuggled into a warm fur-lined coat and flying across the sky behind eight tiny reindeer. Then his mind wandered farther afield to Sam clad in *only* a fur-lined coat, giving him a come-hither look as she lounged on his leather sofa.

Stop! Not the kind of fantasy to have in your head while you're eating breakfast with your four-year-old daughter.

He blinked and refocused. "Why did he do that?"

Ali shrugged. "He knows we need her."

Out of the mouths of babes as Da would've said.

He had no adequate response to that, so he simply said, "Eat your eggs."

"There's white in them." Ali pushed the eggs to the side of her plate and ate another blueberry.

Conor rolled his eyes. She wasn't normally a picky eater, but she hated white in her scrambled eggs. "I beat those eggs to within an inch of their lives, kiddo. The white is cheese.

All I had was pizza cheese."

"Oh, okay." She forked up a pile of fluffy egg and shoved it into her mouth. "We need to go to the grocery store, Da."

"Don't talk with your mouth full." Conor heaved a little sigh of relief that the topic of Sam Hayes had been dropped for the moment because, frankly, he was wondering the same thing his daughter was. When *was* Sam coming home? "Let's go shopping on our way home from school today, okay?"

"Do you have a list?" Ali gazed at him expectantly, looking and sounding so much like her mother that a sweet pang went through him. Sometimes it seemed as though the child was four going on twenty-six.

"I'll start one." He reached behind him to grab the memo pad and pen off the bar and began scribbling, grateful for the distraction.

But his mind was only partially on the grocery list. In the back of his mind floated the beautiful specter of Samantha Hayes and the deadline he'd given himself before he contacted her. *December twenty-fourth.* He'd resisted calling or texting her because something told him to hold off, but the deadline was drawing near, and that little voice was starting to bug him. It might be time to take matters into his own hands.

ELIZABETH HAYES—AUNT BETTE to Sam—was a sight for

sore eyes. Dressed in a Purdue Boilermakers sweatshirt and jeans tucked into red cowboy boots, she bounded down the front steps as Sam pulled into the wide driveway. Bette's silvery-blonde chin-length bob bounced as she trotted beside the car. She yanked the door open as soon as Sam turned off the engine, barely waiting for her to unbuckle her seat belt and hop out before throwing her arms around her in a bear hug. "I've missed the heck outta you! It's been way too long!"

Tears stung Sam's eyes as she returned the embrace. Gosh, how she needed this kind of reception after the last few weeks. "Lord, I'm glad to finally be here." Sam leaned back to give her aunt a smile. The two women had always been almost identical in height and build, but it seemed that her aunt may have shrunk a fraction of an inch. At fifty-three, her green eyes, although still bright and sparkling, were no longer on a level with Sam's own brown ones. But she was slim and straight as an arrow and her arms around Sam's shoulders were still just as strong. It was that strength Sam needed, the unconditional love that her dad's sister had always granted her.

"Want to get unloaded? I've got your room all ready for you. Is that a bag of gifts? Hey wait! I thought we agreed no gifts this year." Bette chattered a mile a minute as she turned away to wrench open the back door of the car.

"Aunt Bette, slow down." Sam stopped her as the older woman pulled out a garment bag and a cooler. "I need to go inside and take a breath, get a glass of water or something . . ."

"How about some wine?" Bette, her arms loaded, still managed to shove the door closed with her hip.

"You just said the magic word. Let's deal with the car later." Frankly, Sam was anxious to get out of the cold weather and into the warmth of the house. A glass of wine sounded pretty darn appealing, too.

"Watch the steps; I salted them, but they can still be slippery." Bette led the way into the big screened porch that spanned the front of her craftsman-style cottage. She had lived here since moving to Primrose, a little town set among the pines just a mile from Lake Michigan. Indiana Dunes State Park was practically in Bette's backyard and Sam had wandered the dunes and the beach every summer until she went to college. The white wicker porch furniture cushioned with faded flowered chintz took her right back to those halcyon days.

From the time she was six years old, her parents had dropped her at Bette's as soon as school let out and didn't return for her until Labor Day. Sam had reveled in lazy summer days, fireflies at dusk, and picnics on the beach, while her parents pursued their own lives in Chicago. Summers with her aunt were magical, and it was Bette who had given Sam a real childhood.

The tension in her shoulders released as she stepped into the house and stopped, closing her eyes to breathe in the scents of Murphy's oil soap, sunshine on linen, and the sage-

and-citrus candles that Aunt Bette burned all day long. A Christmas tree with gaily wrapped packages piled underneath glittered in the corner by the fireplace and Sam spun around to face her aunt with an accusing grin. "Um, looks like I'm not the only one who ignored the no gifts rule."

Bette didn't even bother to look abashed. Instead she lifted her chin. "A Christmas tree looks stupid without gifts under it. Besides, it's nothing fabulous. I saw a couple of things I couldn't resist for you. And you know your mother. She expects gifts at Christmas. Hell, she expects gifts on Arbor Day."

Sam snickered. "I know. I found a gorgeous purse for her at Kate Spade and of course, a bottle of Joy from Neiman Marcus."

"Am I the only one who finds irony in the fact that *your* mother's favorite perfume is called *Joy?*" Bette's eyes twinkled when she glanced back over her shoulder at Sam.

She grinned. "Actually, that particular irony was lost on me until a couple of Christmases ago when I was standing at the perfume counter with my jaw on the floor over an ounce of the stuff in a Baccarat crystal atomizer that had an eighteen-hundred-dollar price tag. Not at all *joy*ful."

"Only Carlynne." Bette shook her head in mock sadness and then hefted the cooler. "What's in here?"

"Water. Iced tea, and a quiche and two pies from Hoosier Mama's. Dutch apple pie and pumpkin cheesecake." She followed Bette into the kitchen, grateful that the remodel her aunt had completed last year didn't change the homey feel of the big room. "I still love what you've done in here!" she exclaimed as Bette unloaded the cooler into her fancy stainless-steel fridge.

Bette pulled a bottle of wine from the wine rack built into the new center island. "Angeline pinot okay?"

"Does it go with apple pie? Because I'm seriously thinking we need pie." Sam settled onto a stool at the island breakfast bar and spun around, admiring the white-washed oak cabinets and the fresh gray granite countertops. Even the old wide-plank oak floor had been refinished to a warm satiny glow.

"Pinot goes with everything." Bette set the pie, two plates, and a pie server in front of Sam. "Cut me a big slice. I only had yogurt for lunch." She brought two wine stems and poured the red wine, then sat down on the stool beside Sam and held up her glass. "To you, kiddo. I couldn't be more pleased to have you here."

"Thanks." Sam clinked glasses and sipped. The pinot was wonderful, but that didn't surprise her. Aunt Bette served excellent wine and food—not particularly gourmet, but always delicious. "You have no idea how grateful I am. I needed to get away."

"Do you want to tell me why you're here two days early or shall we save it until we've had more wine?" Bette emphasized the point by refilling both their glasses.

Sam blinked back the tears that were pressing against her

eyelids and swallowed the bite of pie that had turned to dust in her mouth. It was time to spill the whole story and Aunt Bette was the only person in the world she trusted to help her sort out the mess she'd become since leaving River's Edge.

Chapter Twenty-One

B ETTE SAT PATIENTLY as Sam gazed into her wineglass, trying to decide where to begin. After another sip of wine and a big bite of pie, she blurted, "I think I'm losing it and I'm scared."

"Um . . . I'm probably going to need a little more detail, kid." Bette put her elbow on the bar and rested her chin in her palm. "Can you pin down what makes you think that?"

"I-I sorta had a breakdown during a client meeting and I walked out on them," Sam confessed.

Bette raised one blond brow. "A *breakdown*?"

Sam nodded, chagrined. "I literally screamed at this idiot couple who have been going back and forth over a settlement for months. I kind of told them they were self-centered little babies."

Aunt Bette gave her a suspicious look. "*Kind of* told them?"

Sam sighed. "Okay, I said those exact words. These two have wrangled over the tiniest, stupidest things—not their kids of course. Neither one of them seemed to give a hoot who got custody of their eight-year-old twins, but the BMW, the condo in Miami, and the zero-turn mower were huge bones of contention. This time it was freaking season tickets to the Indy 500. He wanted them so he could take his new squeeze to the race next May. She wasn't budging because she'd promised her new boyfriend those turn four northwest vista seats for the next race. They were fighting and arguing and getting uglier and uglier. His attorney was trying to calm them down and getting nowhere, while I just sat there fuming." She rolled her eyes and took another quick bite of pie. "Usually, I'm cool. I can handle this stupid stuff; I dunno, though. Something in me snapped and I stood up, leaned over the table, and got right in their faces. I told them there were over two hundred and fifty thousand seats at the effing Indianapolis Motor Speedway, so surely there were enough for everyone in the room to have one, but neither one of them deserved so much as a lawn chair in the parking lot. I added that I didn't know how they ever ended up together in the first place, but they deserved each other, and if they were an example of what marriage was all about, I was damn grateful to be single. After that, I picked up my phone and my laptop and walked out the door."

"Good God, child!" Bette exclaimed. "Please tell me you went back to your office and dug out that bottle of tequila I gave you to keep in your bottom desk drawer."

Sam shook her head, heat rising to her cheeks at the memory of the rest of the story. "Nope. I went to my office, grabbed my purse and coat, and just kept walking. Right past reception, into the elevator, and out of the building—all the way to my apartment." She held up her palm. "Oh, I did make one stop on my way home . . . at Hoosier Mama's for pies and quiche."

Bette gaped at her. Clearly she was trying to make sense of her eminently straight-arrow, uber-responsible, workaholic niece raking a client over the coals before walking out of a business meeting.

Sam shrugged at her aunt's astonished gaze. "Then I packed and drove here." She finished her slice of pie, waiting for Bette to say something . . . anything. Although what she was really looking for was *you're not losing it, honey. Life is hard and those people are idiots. Have another piece of pie.*

Bette *did* cut each of them another slice of pie and then emptied the bottle of pinot into Sam's wineglass. When she finally spoke, it wasn't to offer advice or even an opinion. Instead she simply asked, "What happened in River's Edge, Sammi?"

Sam dithered inwardly, trying to come up with a calm sensible answer that might explain her out-of-character behavior. She could blame it on work stress, on the unrelenting tragedy of dealing with divorces and abused spouses and abandoned children. She could claim she'd finally seen enough sadness and she didn't want to be *The Dragon Lady* anymore. That she was burned out and done at the tender age of thirty-two, because all that was true. But the real crux of the matter won out. "I think I fell in love, Aunt Bette."

And she burst into tears.

"Oh, my sweet Sammi. It's finally happened to you, hasn't it?" Bette yanked a napkin from the holder on the bar and offered it to her, then took her hand and led her to the living room and the big overstuffed sofa. She let Sam cry it out while Bette lit a fire in the fireplace and wrapped a warm knitted throw around Sam's shoulders. Plopping down next to her, she slung an arm around her and murmured soothing little comforts.

The storm of weeping finally slowed down and Sam sat up, wiped her eyes, and blew her nose into the napkin Aunt Bette had given her. They sat silently for a few minutes, and she stared into the crackling fire, watching the flames dance and turn all shades of red, orange, and yellow. How safe it was here in Aunt Bette's cozy little cottage with the only person in the world who'd never judged her or found her wanting.

"Okay, that's out of your system," Aunt Bette said with a wry smile. "Why don't you tell me why falling in love with a hot winemaker—I'm assuming we're talking about the hot winemaker, correct?" At Sam's slight nod, she continued, "So why is *that* a tragedy worthy of this level of tears?"

Sam's heart ached so badly she wasn't at all sure she could even talk about Conor, even though her sensible mind knew that processing out loud might help her cope with the yearning that had burned in her soul since the day Conor Flaherty changed her tire. "I can't ever be what he needs.

And I can't bear the thought of causing him or Ali a moment of pain."

"Ali?" Bette rose, collected their wineglasses from the bar, and carried them into the living room. She handed one to Sam. "Who's Ali?"

"Conor's daughter. She's four and an adorable little pixie. But she needs a mom . . ." A lump formed in her throat again. "Oh, Aunt Bette, I have no idea how to be a mother. What if I'm just like my own mother? I've never had a burning desire for children. But, oh man, *this* little girl stole my heart. What if I get involved with him, and then realize I can't do it? It would break her heart. And his. They've had enough sorrow to last a lifetime. They certainly don't need someone like me. A neurotic, overwound mess of a woman." She blinked back tears and stared into her wineglass.

Bette stroked back a tendril of hair that had fallen across Sam's cheek. "You know, I had no idea how to be a mother the first summer a certain six-year-old was dropped on my doorstep. I had to go with my instincts, and there were days I had no clue what to do. So I just loved her and I think it all turned out pretty well." Lifting Sam's chin with one finger, she said, "That little girl went on to be a brilliant attorney and a warm, loving woman, not a neurotic mess." She shook her head and smiled. "Not one bit of a neurotic mess." With a toothy grin, she added, "I'll give you overwound, though. However, take it from me, nothing fixes *that* like life with a kid."

Bette's fond expression caused Sam's heart to fill with tenderness for the woman who had indeed been more of a mother to Sam than her own mother ever thought of being. Not only was she a wonderful friend and companion, but she'd also been the epitome of motherly love, raising Sam every summer with grace and humor and intelligence. Encouraging her to follow her dreams and be her own person, rejoicing in her victories, offering love and sympathy when she was feeling defeated, and always, always dispensing advice with clarity and wisdom.

In a sudden rush of affection, Sam threw her arms around her beloved aunt and hugged her close. "I love you, Aunt Bette." she whispered, her voice choky. "You *are* the best mother in the world."

"You can be, too, if you choose." Aunt Bette leaned back and swiped away the tears on Sam's cheek even though her own eyes were glistening. "And it's not too late for you to have more kids if you—and he—want them."

Sam dropped back against the sofa and tugged the afghan closer around her. "I don't know. Did I tell you he's a widower?" When Bette shook her head, she continued. "That's the other thing. He was . . . *is* so in love with his wife and her illness and death devastated him. He told me she was the light of his life—his words, honest. Her name was Emmy and she was beautiful and amazing. They'd been together forever, Aunt Bette—since they were kids. I don't know how . . . how . . ." She chewed her lower lip for a moment, remembering the light in Conor's eyes when he spoke of Emmy and the photographs all over the house of the two of them, and then the three of them. How could she ever hope to be what he needed when he'd already known that kind of love?

"How you can ever make him *that* happy again." Bette completed the sentence for her.

As usual Bette had nailed it and Sam chuckled grimly through her tears. "I don't know how to be someone's light. How do I live up to a ghost?"

"Did I ever tell you about Joe's first wife?" Bette rose, stirred the fire, and added another log from the canvas holder on the hearth.

Sam shook her head. She had no idea Joe Samuels had ever been married before. He and Bette had been together forever.

Her aunt settled into the armchair next to the sofa. "Her name was Willow. *She* was the light of *his* life. They'd only been married a couple of years when she was killed by a drunk driver in Albuquerque. When I met him, he'd moved to Taos and was selling his paintings and sculptures in a little gallery on the North Plaza. I was there scouting a setting for my next Timothy book. Joe lived above the gallery in a studio apartment. Willow had been gone for just over two years, and his eyes had the hollowed-out look of a refugee. But his art, whew"—she wagged her head and her silvery hair flew across her chin—"he was pouring all his grief into those bronzes and paintings. They were stormy and dark and tragic, but gorgeous, too." She breathed a little laugh. "I was so attracted to them and to him. At first I had a hard time sorting out what I wanted more. The art or the artist. Turns out he was just as drawn to me and fascinated with my Timothy books. He told me about Willow right away, and I could see how much he loved her. Like you, I wondered if I could ever have all of him because it seemed as if a part of him would always belong to her."

"Yes." Sam swallowed as the tears welled up again. "Exactly. If you could've seen his face when he talked about her . . ."

Bette leaned forward, her hands on her knees. "Sammi, listen to me. I finally figured out something important about Joe and Willow and me, and I think you may find the same thing to be true of Conor and Emmy and you."

"What?" Sam sniffled and started to cross her arms over her chest, hoping to ease the ache there.

Instead, Bette reached for Sam's hands, pulling her arms away from her heart and opening her in the space between them. "Emmy is a part of who he is, so you have to invite her to stay, get to know her so you can get to know him. Because of her, Conor is showing you who he is—that he's a good husband and father. That he has staying power. His devotion to Emmy is her gift to you if you let it be. Accept it, build on it. It's not a competition, honey, it's a continuation and if you love him, it will be a completion."

Amazed at the intensity of her aunt's words, Sam laced her fingers with Bette's. "May I ask you something?"

"Ask me anything."

"Why did you and Joe never get married?"

"What makes you think we didn't?" Bette's green eyes twinkled.

Sam gasped. "But . . . but you live here and he lives in Taos . . ." She pointed an accusing finger at her aunt. "You never told me!"

"There are all kinds of marriages, kiddo." Bette squeezed her fingers and released them, settling back into the chair. "Joe's and mine works for us. We're both temperamental artists. We discovered early on that we could never live together, so once a month or so, one of us gets on a plane or we meet halfway. And you know, Joe's paintings began to lighten up the longer we were together. Color came back to his life and his work and he brought new life to me and mine. Yeah, we live apart, but you know, it's always a honeymoon when we get together, and that works for us." She smiled, contentment obvious on her lined face. "You and Conor will find what works for you. But, *first*, you have to go to him and give this thing a chance."

Sam's heart rose as she gazed into her aunt's sweet face. She *could* go to him, at least spend the holidays in River's Edge and see what might be possible. A shiver of excitement raced through her. If she left after breakfast tomorrow, she could be there by early afternoon—in time for Christmas

Eve with them. She already had the perfect gift for Conor—a beautiful book on the history of winemaking that she'd found in the Barnes and Noble on Jackson. She'd bought it, knowing she'd never see Conor again, but when she opened the big volume and saw the gorgeous color illustrations, she'd pulled out her VISA card without even thinking. She'd taken it out again at Macy's when she found a set of four elegant Waterford crystal wine stems while she was shopping for her mother. At the time, she'd convinced herself they were for Bette, but in her heart, they were Conor's. Irish crystal for her Irish winemaker.

She clenched her fingers together. All she needed was a gift for Ali. Then it struck her; the little girl had been fascinated by Sam's bracelet-style activity monitor. She could run by Target and get the child's version for Ali, then wrap her gifts and be on her way in the morning.

With a joyous cry, she threw her arms around Bette. "I'm going to him," she declared and for the first time since David had taken back his ring and she'd danced on the beach in the moonlight, Samantha Hayes was sure of exactly what she wanted.

Chapter Twenty-Two

CONOR CARRIED A giant platter of ham to the already groaning serving table in the tasting room and set it down between Teresa's cheesy potato casserole and Brendan's special organic glazed carrots. They'd opted to have a luncheon Christmas Eve celebration up at the winery because Conor couldn't stop inviting townsfolk to join them. Eventually they simply had too many guests for his house or Char's to accommodate. But a fire crackled merrily in the big stone fireplace and the Christmas tree twinkled in the corner nearby. Ali couldn't stay away from the stack of gifts that surrounded the tall Douglas fir. The scents of pine, woodsmoke, and great food filled the air, and the room rang with laughter and chatter.

Sean stood behind the tasting bar opening bottles of chilled chardonnay and Conor's new Gewürztraminer, which had already gotten rave reviews from all three of his brothers as well as Charlotte. Megan Mackenzie set out stemmed glasses while she teased Sean as she had ever since they were all kids together. Brendan and Tierney Ashton were deep in conversation as they laid out stacks of plates and utensils, and

Aidan flirted with sixty-year-old Paula Meadows as she opened box after box of goodies from her bakery, including a decorated Christmas cake that she'd made especially for "her boys" from Maggie Flaherty's recipe. Paula playfully slapped Aidan's hand away when he tried to scoop up a fingerful of frosting.

Conor grabbed a glass of Gewürztraminer and gazed with affection at the crowd of friends and family gathered in the winery, grateful again for the support and love that surrounded him in this small river town. They'd all rallied 'round him when Emmy had gotten sick, provided unfailing comfort when she'd died, and had been ever-present even when Conor himself had not been present at all. They'd watched, fascinated, when Sam Hayes brought him back to the land of the living, so they were invested in how he intended to get her back to River's Edge. Several people had already asked about her, making not-at-all-subtle remarks about how he needed to get it in gear and go find her.

Mac, who had closed the diner for Christmas, sauntered over to the bar with a couple of bottles of Maréchal Foch and zinfandel for Sean to open. The chef did love his dry reds. "So, kid, what's the good word?" Mac eyed Sean as he uncorked the foch and poured several glasses. He nabbed one, took a sip, and closed his eyes in obvious appreciation. "Conor Flaherty, you make fine wine, now. Don't ever let anyone tell you different."

Conor glanced at the bottle sitting behind the bar. "Thanks, but that one's Da's. *My* foch is still in the barrel."

Mac shrugged. "You learned at the foot of the master. I'm sure yours will be amazing, too. Nice thing is I'll be here to give *it* a try and *you* an opinion."

"I can always count on you, Mac." Conor tossed him a grin.

"Have I told you how great it is to see you back among us?" Mac returned the smile and leaned his elbows on the bar. "We've all missed you. Missed *this*." He waved an all-encompassing hand in both silent and eloquent acknowledgement of the joyful group gathered before them.

Gratitude overwhelmed Conor again. "I kept thinking, especially these past few weeks, what Emmy would have said to me." He grinned. "Actually, she wouldn't have said anything. She would've just smacked me upside the head. I squandered too much time these past couple of years. Ali turned into a little girl and I almost missed it, Mac."

"Welcome back," Mac said simply and offered his glass up as a toast. "And, man, don't beat yourself up; you're doing a good job. That kid is a little charmer."

Their gazes went to Alannah, who was busy showing Nate Ashton the presents under the tree, pointing out one in particular that had his name on it. Conor had picked up a new wallet to replace the tattered one that Nate always carried, then tucked an iTunes gift card inside from Ali. She was more excited about the others opening their gifts than she was about the stuff waiting for her under their tree at the house. Mac gave him a thumbs-up and wandered over to sit at a table with Dot and Mary Higgins, who were enjoying the new Gewürztraminer.

Conor stepped behind the bar with Sean as Megan slid away to join her dad and the Higgins sisters. He raised his hand to wave Aidan and Brendan over. "Everybody's here, so I think we're ready to eat."

Sean tapped on a wineglass with a spoon to get the room's attention while Aidan clapped his hands. When everyone was focused on Sean, he cleared his throat. "Wow, how great is it to be together again for Christmas? We haven't done this in a couple of years and I know Da would be delighted to see the tasting room all decorated for the holidays and full of family and friends—especially *this* year."

"Yeah, I'm sure he and Ma and Emmy are smiling and dancing up there in heaven," Aidan added as he slung an arm around Conor's shoulders.

After a nanosecond of dead silence, Conor chuckled and kissed the top of his little brother's head. "I sure hope so, Little Brother. We need more dancing—here and in heaven. Merry Christmas, everyone!"

The room exploded into joyful laughter and applause that lasted so long, it took Sean nearly a full minute to quiet the group for a blessing of gratitude for the food and the fellowship.

HIS BELLY STUFFED, Conor gazed around the table he was sitting at with his brothers and recalled, for a moment, the last dinner they'd shared only a month ago. Thanksgiving had been a grim meal as they discussed how they were going to deal with Charlotte's lawsuit and what would happen if they lost the contest of their father's will. He'd started that day gloomy anyway, missing Emmy and Da and Char, and all the fun the four of them used to have in the kitchen, preparing the turkey and all the fixings that went with it. He'd gone to bed that night more depressed than usual as the heavy fear for his family's winery weighed on his mind and heart. Emmy hadn't been there to snuggle with him and assure him in her inimitable sunny way that everything would be fine.

Then he stopped for a beautiful drenched woman on the side of Drury Road and a light turned on his life. Was Samantha Hayes the slap upside the head that he'd joked about with Mac earlier? He smiled at the image in his head of a winged Emmy Flaherty reaching down from the clouds to flatten Sam's tire, knowing he would pull over to help. *Anything is possible*—those words had become his new mantra. *Anything is possible.* He'd been repeating them to himself since the day Sam walked out of the diner.

"What're you grinning about?" Bren nudged him with his elbow before taking another bite of cake and washing it down with a sip of Gewürztraminer. "Man, Paula nailed Mom's Christmas cake, didn't she?"

Conor loved how his uber-health-conscious brother was eating everything on the dessert table without a moment of hesitation. Locked away in an office somewhere in Washington, DC, doing Lord-knew-what for the CIA, Bren sometimes missed the really good stuff in life, like wonderful food and perfect wine and an actual social life. "I'm just glad to see you eating cake for a change instead of only going for the fruit plate. Nothing wrong with fruit, mind you, but cake is life, big brother, and you need to start living it."

Sean snorted, then snickered. "Um, speaking of living life, Conny, can we talk about this attorney I know who is a complete basket case?"

Conor couldn't hide his delighted grin. "She is?"

"She went off on a client and walked out of a meeting." Sean peered at him over the top of his glasses. "Not that I blamed her. Those people are asses, but she never, ever lets her emotions show. She's The Dragon Lady—always cool and collected. Suddenly she's storming into the elevator without so much as a *kiss my butt* or *see you later*."

"Sam did that?" Conor was astounded and overjoyed. She was as upside down as he was and that had to mean something good.

"Yup."

"Sounds like a lady in love to me." Bren snaked his fork out, going for the icing Aidan had scraped off his cake and left on the side of his plate.

Aidan shoved the dish closer to him with a little eye roll. "Just take it, Mr. Natural." He focused on Conor. "What are you going to do about her?"

"I've been giving her time. It felt like the right thing to do. This hit us like a comet and she ran scared." Conor took a long deep breath and then slowly let it go. "I sorta hoped she'd contact me before we got to the deadline I'd given her in my head."

"Never give a woman a deadline," Bren said sagely, even though he looked rather foolish with red icing on his chin.

Aidan tossed him a napkin. "What do you know about women, you big geek? I'm pretty sure your last date was when you took your best friend's little sister to the eighth-grade dance because some brat stood her up."

"Do I hear my past being taken in vain over there?" Tierney Ashton called from her table a couple of yards away. "And don't diss Bren for saving me all those years ago; he's still my hero."

Brendan blew her a kiss. "Thank you, Tee."

"Daddy, when is Santa coming?" Ali leaned so far back in her chair that Charlotte had to scramble to rescue her. "You said he was coming to our party today."

Conor tossed his stepmother a grateful smile. How good it was to have the family back to normal again. "Honey, he's coming. I'm just not sure when. He's got a lot to do today." With a glance at the clock, he nudged Aidan under the table.

It was almost two and although his village guests were still laughing and eating, he was sure everyone had other places to be on Christmas Eve.

Aidan had agreed to play the jolly old elf at today's festivities and had even brought a darned authentic-looking costume, beard, and real belly stuffing from the studio costume shop in LA. Conor had been impressed when Aidan modeled it earlier while Ali was over at Char's wrapping gifts. The suit was down in the cellar waiting for him. He scooted off his chair and slipped out the front door of the winery with a cheery, "Gotta run to the house, I forgot my gifts! Char, I'm taking your golf cart, okay?"

He and Conor had arranged everything. Aidan would go through the back door downstairs and don the Santa suit; then he'd come back around and make his entrance at the front door. He had to give his actor brother credit; nobody would've guessed he wasn't headed up to the house. Mentioning Char's golf cart was a stroke of acting genius. Ali wasn't going to suspect his absence for one second.

Busy righting Ali in her chair and encouraging the little girl to finish her lunch, Char waved to him. "Keys are on the roof. Help yourself."

Brendan scowled as he wiped the icing from his beard. "I date," he said, proving he hadn't allowed the interruption to eliminate his chance to protest. Sean and Conor just gazed at him. "I do . . . sometimes," he added sheepishly.

"We're not talking about you; we're talking about Conny," Sean reminded him with another of his big-brother, over-the-top-of-his-glasses looks that reminded Conor so much of Da, it gave him a little pang.

"We're not talking about me," he said, his eyes on Ali as she grudgingly finished the last of her ham and green beans.

"What's your deadline?" Sean asked, ignoring him completely.

Conor raked his fingers through his too-long hair—he still hadn't found time for a haircut even though he'd meant to make an appointment with Kari at Shear Magic. His hair was well over his collar. If Da were here, he'd be teasing him about braiding it like Ali's. He bit his lip and sighed. "Today."

"Have you contacted her at all? Texted her? Called her?" Sean poured himself another glass of wine from the bottle in the center of the table. "You must be planning something because I noticed you've been sipping on the same glass of wine all afternoon."

"Not yet. I'm not doing this by phone." He slumped a little, resting his head on his palm. "I can hardly sit still, thinking about driving up and getting her. I know her. I saw how happy she was here. If she came back, we'd have a chance—"

"Why do you think she left?" Brendan, ever the researcher, interrupted.

"I know *exactly* why she left," Conor replied. "She's worried that she and I will never have what Emmy and I had."

"It's a valid concern." Bren tipped the last of the wine into his own glass. "You two were pretty much a picture-perfect marriage."

"No marriage is perfect, but Emmy and I worked, and I want that again," Conor said, his heart lightening at that thought of sharing his life with Sam. "I don't expect Sam and me to be just like Emmy and me, but I have to show her that I want her and that what she and I can have will be just right for us."

His brothers stared at him, clearly dumbfounded at the change in him since Thanksgiving. Heck, Conor was pretty astonished himself. He didn't give all the credit for his turnaround to Sam's arrival, but that was the catalyst and the reason he was so determined to find out what was possible with her.

"Well, dude, it's only four and a half hours to Chicago from here," Brendan finally said as he finished his cake, although he was still eyeing the dessert end of the table.

"She's not in Chicago," Sean said quietly.

"Where is she?" Conor's heart rose to his throat. "Is she okay?" Sean had said Sam was a mess. What if something had happened to her? His heart ached at the thought of her depressed and lonely, especially at Christmas.

"She texted me yesterday. She's at her aunt's house in Primrose, up by the dunes." Sean held up his phone. "I have the address right here."

Chapter Twenty-Three

"I WANT TO go, but what about Ali?" Conor's mind was whirling, even as he nabbed Sean's phone and typed the Primrose, Indiana, address into Google Maps on his own phone. He could drive to Primrose and be back with Sam by midnight, but Ali needed to hang her stocking and leave cookies and milk for Santa.

Sean waved away his concern. "We'll take care of Ali. Just go, man. What's left? Supper? PJs? Bedtime story? Char can braid her hair, and we'll let Aidan read *'Twas the Night Before Christmas* to her."

Conor nodded, only half listening as he sorted through all that needed to happen for Ali to have a merry Christmas Eve. He was more than a little dazed that he was even considering leaving, but he was certain Sam would be the best gift he could possibly give his daughter . . . and himself. "Okay, stockings for all six of us are in the cupboard by the fireplace and there's an extra one. Hang it for Sam. Ali will show you the special plate and cup for Santa's cookies and milk. Don't forget the carrots for Rudolph, although I'm pretty sure she won't let you. She needs to pee and brush her teeth before bed, but Char knows the routine." He pushed his chair away and stood up.

"We've got this, Con." Brendan rose too and hugged him. "Go kiss your daughter good-bye and get outta here."

Apparently, Ali had been listening from the next table because when Conor slipped over to tell her what was happening, she laughed. "Da, wait. Santa will be here soon and he's bringing Sam with him." She gave him a questioning look. "Don't you 'member I dreamed that?"

"That was just a dream, honey." Conor kissed her hair, inhaling the sweet little-girl scent of her, praying he was doing the right thing. "I'm going to go get Sam. I'll be back after you fall asleep, but we'll both be here in the morning." He added under his breath, "I hope."

He dashed to the office to grab his coat and gloves, only vaguely aware of the murmuring of his guests. Sean would explain and he had no doubt he had the blessing of the entire town of River's Edge anyway. Shrugging into his jacket, he felt in his pockets for his car keys and made sure he had his wallet as he stopped for a moment at the front door to zip up his coat.

When he opened the door, his heart stuttered and his knees went weak. Santa Claus was on the deck outside and beside him stood Sam Hayes, looking gorgeous, her arms laden with festive packages, her face wreathed in smiles. Her hair shone in the Christmas lights and her eyes glowed amber brown. "You-you're here," he stammered.

"Merry Christmas, Conor Flaherty." She handed her packages to Aidan, whose grin showed under his impeccable white moustache and beard. Inanely, Conor wondered if it truly *was* Aidan under all those whiskers and the extra belly covered in red velour. But there wasn't time to think as Sam stepped forward into the door and placed one hand on his chest. Somehow he managed not to stumble as she gently propelled him backward a few feet, her eyes locked with his.

When she stopped and glanced up, he lifted his gaze from her beautiful face to see the infamous mistletoe hanging above their heads. Without a moment's hesitation, she framed his face with her hands and drew his mouth down to hers. The kiss lingered longer than it probably should have in front of a room full of people, but Conor didn't care. He wrapped his arms around her and got lost in the intoxication of Sam's kiss.

He pressed his cheek to hers, and when she spoke, her breath stirred the hair that fell over his ear, making him tremble with delight. "Let's give this thing a chance, okay?"

Smiling at the tears glistening in her eyes, he nodded. "Anything is possible, Sam Hayes. Anything at all."

"Sam!" They turned at the elated screech and the patter of little feet across the wide-plank floor. "See, Da?" Ali exclaimed. "I told you! He brought her. I knew he'd bring her!" She threw her arms around Sam's legs and Sam picked her up to hug her close. Ali snuggled into her arms and blew a kiss over Sam's shoulder to Santa, who looked very dapper leaning against the doorframe, his arms crossed over his round stomach. "Thank you, Santa! Thank you!"

"Ho, ho, ho, Ali Flaherty." Aidan's belly laugh deepened a full register lower than usual. "Merry Christmas, little one."

Conor glanced around the room happily, but his gaze was snagged when one of the embellished white berries dropped off the sprig of mistletoe and fell into Sam's hair, shimmering there like a pearl. His eyes filled with tears of joy as he put his arms around Sam and Ali.

"Thanks, Emmy," he whispered and then kissed Sam full on the lips amid the raucous cheers and applause of his friends and family.

Epilogue

"**H**APPY NEW YEAR, kiddo." Harry Evans swooped Sam into a bear hug and swung her around with a strength that surprised the heck out of her.

"Happy New Year, Harry." Sam pecked him on the cheek before the two of them settled into stools at one of the square tables in the winery tasting room. It was after midnight and most of the guests had already left, but Harry had hung around to help with clean-up.

Once again, friends and family had gathered at Four Irish Brothers to celebrate, and once again, Harry Evans was late to the party. Just one of the many little quirks that had endeared River's Edge to Sam in the days since she'd returned. Rose had welcomed her with open arms and given her the same room she'd had before, complete with a charming swag of fresh pine across the fireplace mantel that made the room smell lovely and seem even cozier.

Harry held up his wineglass and tipped it toward her. "To the new year. May it bring you all your heart desires."

Sam smiled, touched her glass to his, and took a sip of Conor's excellent sparkling Traminette, his own take on the official grape of Indiana. It was crisp and delicious and just as he advertised on the big blackboard by the door, *THE PERFECT WINE TO TOAST IN THE NEW YEAR.*

"Same to you, Harry."

He leaned back in his chair and eyed her with a look that Sam couldn't decipher. "So what's next?" he asked.

"*I'm* what's next," Conor piped up as he pulled out the stool opposite Harry's, plopped into it, and reached for Sam's hand. His blue eyes glowed sapphire in the lights high above them, while the candlelight on the table cast flickering shadows across his handsome face. "Well, me and that little imp over there trying to charm another piece of cake out of her grandmother." He nodded in the direction of the nearly empty serving table. "Let her have a little piece, Char, it's okay," he called with an exaggerated eye roll. "She's already so ramped up, a little more sugar isn't going to make a bit of difference. She'll drop like a rock in a little while."

"*You're* what's next?" Harry raised one bushy white brow, skeptically.

"You don't really think she came back for you, do you, old man?" Conor winked and flashed Sam a smile so sexy, it nearly took her breath away.

Harry grinned and shot Conor a quick middle finger. "Actually, that's exactly what I intend to talk to her about."

"Well, she and I are working on a plan, so no interference from you, okay?" Conor returned the middle finger and Harry chortled.

"I think she might want to consider what I'm going to offer." He puffed out his chest and looked down his nose at Conor.

"Sitting right here." Sam reminded them as she laced her fingers with Conor's, basking in the warmth of his big hand on hers. "Stop talking about me like I'm invisible, please."

She and Conor *had* talked . . . endlessly since she'd arrived on Christmas Eve. He'd told her he was willing to do whatever she wanted, even if it meant a long-distance relationship for a while with Skype calls between Chicago and River's Edge and occasional in-person weekends. He couldn't leave Four Irish Brothers and she never imagined he would, but equally, he declared he was proud of her success and assumed she'd want her burgeoning career at Stark, Randolph, Smith, and Flaherty to keep flourishing. They would make it work, he'd reassured her time and again.

On the other hand, Sam continued to fall in love with the little river town and all its citizens. She'd already bought a beautiful quilt from Dot and Mary Higgins for Aunt Bette's fifty-fourth birthday coming up in January, taken Ali to the steamboat museum, and had omelets with Megan at Mac's. Megan's enthusiasm for converting the old Parrish cotton mill—one of the last remaining examples of the industrial waterfront left along the mighty Ohio—into condos was contagious. The two of them had talked for hours one morning during a long breakfast, with Sam making copious notes and thinking the project just might intrigue her mother, who regularly took on fundraising for worthy causes in Chicago. She'd surprised herself with that thought, but somehow even working on her relationship with her distant mother had become more palatable in River's Edge.

Fact was she wanted to stay in River's Edge, be with Conor and Ali, and help him in his work. But she didn't want to give up her career as an attorney. She'd worked too hard to get where she was. Was she ready to give up the lucrative practice in Chicago where the possibility of becoming a partner in a few years loomed large? Although, after her rather humiliating lack of professionalism with the Franklins, she was no longer quite so confident of a permanent spot in the Stark, Randolph lineup. Sean had been uncharacteristically silent about that particular debacle in the week they'd both been down in River's Edge.

"Remember I told you that I had something I needed your help with?" Harry leaned forward, folding his hands on the table.

Sam nodded. "How can I help you?"

"I'm going to run for circuit court judge, so I need to find an attorney to handle my practice. It's not big-city lawyering; mostly family stuff and some contracts and the occasional DUI. Nothing sexy like what you're used to, but you've got good knowledge of the law and a heart full of compassion. That's what it takes. Would you consider it?"

Sam's heart thumped in her chest and tears stung her

eyes. For the very first time in her adult life—heck, maybe in her entire life, she'd acted entirely spontaneously when she'd gotten into her car and driven down to River's Edge. No plan, no idea what to expect; just a huge ache for Conor Flaherty and a driving need to see Ali. Harry's offer gave her the opportunity she needed to begin a new life here.

But before she could open her mouth to respond, Sean spoke up from behind her. "Harry, you old dog, are you stealing my associate?"

"I'm tryin'." Harry confessed. "Comes with an apartment, Sam. A nice little two-bedroom unit above my offices. Has a great view of the river. Might need a little update, but I'm sure Conor and the boys would help you get it into shape."

Sean slipped into the seat across from Sam. "I can arrange for you to have a leave from the firm if you want to help him out for a while, Sam."

A *leave*? Sam tightened her hold on Conor's fingers and met his steady gaze across the table. Although his expression remained impassive, his blue eyes were filled with anticipation. She took a deep breath. "Thank you, Sean, but no. I don't want a leave. I'm offering you my resignation from the firm right here, right now. A formal letter will be on your desk January fifth—as soon as we get back to Chicago."

She held her breath, expecting Sean to argue with her, but instead he broke into a wide grin that turned into a chuckle. "I had a feeling that would be your answer." He patted Conor on the shoulder. "If you weren't my little brother, I'd deck you for taking away one of my best associates. But, to tell you the truth, I've never seen her so happy and contented and I'm pretty sure that's all on you, Bro."

Conor turned his delicious smile on Sam and when he brought her hand up to his lips and pressed a kiss into her palm, she nearly melted in her chair. "Not just me, big brother—I had some help." He grinned as Ali flew across the room, her face covered in icing.

"Da!" She hurled herself into his arms before he could grab a napkin to wipe her chin. "Did you ask her?" She settled her tiny body in his lap and put both hands on his face, forcing him to look her in the eyes. "Did you?"

"You're pushing, poppet. I told you *I'd* know when the time is right." He swiped at her cheeks and lips with a napkin he'd dipped in his water glass. Then he wiped her fingers and his own face, so comfortable with the little ritual that it seemed as though he didn't even notice Sam gazing at him. Warmth flooded through her as she realized again what a great father he was, how naturally parenting came to him. He could teach her, help her find her way to the instincts she believed without a doubt were in her as well.

"But she's leaving soon and we can't let her leave!"

"If you're talking about me, little one, I'm not leaving." Sam reached her arms out and took Ali from Conor, cuddling her close. "At least not forever. Harry just offered me a job and I think I'm going to say yes."

"Then you can marry us." Ali's dark eyes sparkled with honey lights.

"Ali . . ." Conor gave her a dad-warning look that Sam found incredibly hot, but didn't seem to dissuade his daughter one bit.

Ali shrugged and raised her palms in obvious frustration. "I'm tired of waiting for you to know when it's the right time; you're taking forever!" she said, her little voice full of indignation.

Sam chuckled, but then caught Conor staring at her, an odd, but tender expression on his face. "You know what?" he said, keeping his eyes locked with Sam's over Ali's dark head. "You're right, poppet. What do you say, Sam? Will you marry me . . . us?"

Sam's heart soared and she drew Ali closer as Conor leaned in. "Anything is possible, Conor Flaherty. Anything at all," she said. And when his lips met hers, Ali obligingly lowered her head to Sam's shoulder to give them room for a heart-stopping kiss.

The End

Don't miss the next book in Nan Reinhardt's
Four Irish Brother Winery series!

Coming soon!

More charming holiday stories from Tule Publishing

Rescued by Christmas by Erika Marks

Wedding at the Mistletoe Chalet by Dani Collins

A Merry Mountain Christmas by Trish Milburn

The Christmas Window by Melissa McClone

Available now at your favorite online retailer!

About the Author

Nan Reinhardt has been a copy editor and proofreader for over twenty-five years, and currently works mainly on fiction titles for a variety of clients, including Avon Books, St. Martin's Press, Kensington Books, Tule Publishing, and Entangled Publishing, as well as for many indie authors.

Author Nan writes romantic fiction for women in their prime. Yeah, women still fall in love and have sex, even after they turn forty-five! Imagine! She is also a wife, a mom, a mother-in-law, and a grandmother. She's been an antiques dealer, a bank teller, a stay-at-home mom, and a secretary.

She loves her career as a freelance editor, but writing is Nan's first and most enduring passion. She can't remember a time in her life when she wasn't writing—she wrote her first romance novel at the age of ten, a love story between the most sophisticated person she knew at the time, her older sister (who was in high school and had a driver's license!), and a member of Herman's Hermits. If you remember who they are, *you* are Nan's audience! She's still writing romance, but now from the viewpoint of a wiser, slightly rumpled, post-menopausal woman who believes that love never ages, women only grow more interesting, and everybody needs a little sexy romance.

Visit Nan's website at www.nanreinhardt.com, where you'll find links to all her books as well as blogs about writing, being a Baby Boomer, and aging gracefully . . . mostly. Nan also blogs every Tuesday at Word Wranglers, sharing the spotlight with four other romance authors; and she is a regular contributor at the Romance University website, where she blogs as Nan Reinhardt, Copy Editor. Her latest novel, *Saving Sarah*, book 4 in the Women of Willow Bay series released September 26, 2017.

Thank you for reading

A Small Town Christmas

If you enjoyed this book, you can find more from all our great authors at TulePublishing.com, or from your favorite online retailer.

TULE
PUBLISHING

Printed in the USA
CPSIA information can be obtained
at www.ICGtesting.com
LVHW042203261123
764993LV00008B/227